NEXUS CONFESSIONS:
VOLUME FOUR

NEXUS CONFESSIONS: VOLUME FOUR

Edited and compiled by
Lindsay Gordon
and Lance Porter

In real life, make sure you practise safe,
sane and consensual sex.

First published in 2008 by
Nexus
Thames Wharf Studios
Rainville Rd
London W6 9HA

A catalogue record for this book is available from the
British Library.

www.nexus-books.com

Typeset by TW Typesetting, Plymouth, Devon
Printed and bound in Great Britain by
CPI Bookmarque, Croydon, CR0 4TD

Distributed in the USA by Macmillan, 175 Fifth Avenue,
New York, NY 10010, USA

ISBN 978 0 352 34136 5

Mixed Sources
Product group from well-managed
forests and other controlled sources
www.fsc.org Cert no. TT-COC-2139
© 1996 Forest Stewardship Council

FSC

The Random House Group Limited supports The Forest
Stewardship Council [FSC], the leading international forest
certification organisation. All our titles that are printed on
Greenpeace approved FSC certified paper carry the FSC logo.
Our paper procurement policy can be found at
www.rbooks.co.uk/environment

1 3 5 7 9 10 8 6 4 2

CONTENTS

Introduction

Who can forget the first time they read a reader's letter in an adult magazine? It could make your legs shake. You could almost feel your imagination stretching to comprehend exactly what some woman had done with a neighbour, the baby-sitter, her best friend, her son's friend, a couple of complete strangers, whatever . . . Do real women actually do these things? Did this guy really get that lucky? We asked ourselves these questions, and the not knowing, and the wanting to believe, or wanting to disbelieve because we felt we were missing out, were all part of the reading experience, the fun, the involvement in the confessions of others, as if we were reading some shameful diary. And when Nancy Friday's collections of sexual fantasies became available, didn't we all shake our heads and say, no way, some depraved writer made all of this up. No woman could possibly want to do that. Or this guy must be crazy. But I bet there are reader's letters and confessed fantasies that we read years, even decades ago, that we can still remember clearly. Stories that haunt us: did it, might it, could it have really happened? And stories that still thrill us when the lights go out because they have informed our own dreams. But as we get older and become more experienced, maybe we have learnt that we would be foolish to underestimate anyone sexually, especially ourselves.

The scope of human fantasy and sexual experience seems infinite now. And our sexual urges and imaginations never cease to eroticise any new situation or trend or cultural flux about us. To browse online and to see how many erotic sub-cultures have arisen and made themselves known, is to be in awe. Same deal with magazines and adult films – the variety, the diversity, the complexity and level of obsessive detail involved. But I still believe there are few pictures or visuals that can offer the insights into motivation and desire, or reveal the inner world of a fetish, or detail the pure visceral thrill of sexual arousal, or the anticipation and suspense of a sexual experience in the same way that a story can. When it comes to the erotic you can't beat a narrative, and when it comes to an erotic narrative you can't beat a confession. An actual experience or longing confided to you, the reader, in a private dialogue that declares: *yes, if I am honest, I even shock myself at what I have done and what I want to do.* There is something comforting about it. And unlike a novel, with an anthology there is the additional perk of dipping in and out and of not having to follow continuity; the chance to find something fresh and intensely arousing every few pages written by a different hand. Start at the back if you want. Anthologies are perfect for erotica, and they thrive when the short story in other genres has tragically gone the way of poetry.

So sit back and enjoy the Nexus Confessions series. It offers the old-school thrills of reading about the sexual shenanigans of others, but Nexus-style. And the fantasies and confessions that came flooding in – when the call went out on our website – are probably only suitable for Nexus. Because like the rest of our canon, they detail fetishes, curious tastes and perverse longings: the thrills of shame and humiliation, the swapping of genders, and the ecstasy of submission or domination. There are no visiting milkmen, or busty neighbours hanging out the washing and winking over the hedge here. Oh, no. Our readers and fantasists are far more likely to have been spanked, or caned, feminised into women, have given themselves to strangers, to have dominated other men or women, gone dogging, done the unthinkable, behaved inappropriately and broken the rules.

Lindsay Gordon, Autumn 2006

Symbols key

 Corporal Punishment

 Female Domination

 Institution

 Medical

 Period Setting

 Restraint/Bondage

 Rubber/Leather

 Spanking

 Transvestism

 Underwear

 Uniforms

Losing My Virginity

I had only finished school at the end of July and, a week later, I was busy scrolling through the houses for sale on the computer in the office at Drew-Butler, the estate agents in Canterbury. Father played golf with Peter Drew and, with Father's commitment to the work ethic, I was spending a month of my holidays learning the art of customer relations. I wasn't even being paid but would earn a commission if I sold a property.

Like anyone with any sense, Stuart Butler was on holiday, and Mr Drew was with a client when a man strode into the office with a broad smile on his lips and a heavy bag over his shoulder. He was wearing jeans and a faded denim shirt with too many buttons undone, a decidedly un-Canterbury-like gold chain nestling in the dark hair of his chest. He was about forty, which seemed awfully old to me at the time, with twinkling blue eyes that settled on me with such intensity a flush raced over my neck.

He had seen in the window Black Spires, a big old white elephant of a house for sale outside the village of Ickham. Could he see it now before he took the train back to London? I panicked. Mr Drew had told me he didn't want to be disturbed, but I plucked up the courage and tapped on his door. He looked most put out as I poked my head inside.

1

'Someone wants to see Black Spires.'

'Can you deal with that yourself, my dear?'

'Yes, I suppose . . .'

I closed the door, collected the house keys and followed the man out into the hot afternoon sunshine. We introduced ourselves as we crossed the road to the car park: Milly Edwards, I said.

'Charlie Rolfe. It's a pleasure,' he replied.

He held the car door open for me, the sudden touch of his hand on my arm making me lurch forward against the steering wheel. I felt silly and self-conscious as I repositioned the rear-view mirror and turned the ignition key. He swung his bag on the back seat. He buckled himself in beside me and, as I touched the accelerator, the engine seemed to throb with vague impatience. There was a heat haze rising off the cement and I lowered the window to get some air as I joined the afternoon traffic.

'Is that all right?' I said.

'Yes, I like it,' he replied.

I had only recently passed my test and drove through the villages dotting the countryside with lips tightly closed, hands at ten to two on the steering wheel. I could feel his eyes on me, on my neck with its splash of colour, my bare thighs, on my breasts pushing against the fabric of my blouse, my body under his inspection growing damp with confusion and embarrassment.

As I changed gear he watched my feet dancing over the pedals, my pink skirt riding higher, my nipples growing hard, and I remembered putting on my bra that morning after the shower, staring at myself in the mirror, then taking it off again. I squeezed my nipples until the sting made me grip my teeth in bliss and then with those buds smarting and raw I wriggled into the smallest, skimpiest, most immodest little white blouse in

2

the drawer. I had yet to sell a property and had set out for work that morning with determination in my step and an unexpected dampness between my legs.

'Do you like being an estate agent?' he asked.

'It's only temporary,' I replied.

'Ah, yes. The only permanence is change,' he remarked, his deep voice reminding me of the Bishop who had once given out books and trophies on prize day.

He was turned sideways in his seat, blatantly examining my neck, and my breasts so immodestly prominent with the seat belt dividing them. His eyes undressed me and the shameful thing was I liked it. My little fantasy before the bathroom mirror wasn't exactly a first, it was becoming a ritual. I felt like a drug addict driven by unfulfilled and inexplicable desires. Childhood is like a prison sentence. School was behind me and I felt like a freed slave shaking off my shackles ready to run barefoot into the future.

I steered the car through apple orchards and strawberry fields. In the rush to get out of the office I had forgotten my sunglasses and the intense light made me squint as the car left the shade and entered the sunshine. Flies tapped against the windscreen. We reached a hairpin bend at the bottom of a hill and took a sharp turn onto an unmarked lane easy to miss unless you knew where you were going.

The lane rose above meadows lined with mature oaks before dipping down and rising again to a circular plane where Black Spires sat incongruously on the summit. The dip in the land formed a natural defence. I told Mr Rolfe there had been a building on this spot since the Renaissance.

'That's when it all began,' he remarked.

'Yes, I suppose,' I replied, and felt foolish for saying it.

I turned through the black iron gates and the Mini crunched over a gravel drive edged by rhododendrons and shaded by sycamores. He followed me through an entrance laid out with stone flags below an arcaded roof. The slit windows softened the light and a delicious chill rose from the floor and ran up my skirt. I should have been putting Mr Rolfe at ease, talking about the south-facing aspect and the cellar with its ancient artefacts, but he could see those things without me describing them, and I discerned in Mr Rolfe no desire for the mundane and prosaic. There were butterflies in my tummy and my dark hair felt heavy and damp on my shoulders.

He gazed around the entrance hall for just a moment and I gazed at him. Charlie Rolfe had the most striking blue eyes I had ever seen; sapphire eyes, not like the southern sky, more like two creatures from the depths of a tropical sea. His features were solid, suntanned, his nose large and dominant, his lips full and sensual, his wavy dark hair flecked with silver strands that glimmered in the diffused light.

Our eyes met and I trembled for some reason. My throat was dry and my breasts were betraying me as they pressed painfully against the thin white shirt.

'Would you like to see the drawing room?' I asked.

'I want to see everything,' he replied, and held my eyes until I glanced away.

I felt confused. Perhaps mesmerised was more accurate. Being alone with this stranger with strange blue eyes in this strange house seemed oddly romantic in my schoolgirl mind, and I couldn't remember ever having been in a similar situation before. I didn't know what to expect, what to say, how to behave. All I did know was that I felt light-headed and liberated. Mr Rolfe was still gazing at me, measuring me as if for a new dress. Or no dress at all. My senses were drugged but in the midst of my confusion I felt that there was a connection between us, an indiscernible thread like the strings the puppeteer pulls to guide and manoeuvre the marionette.

Had we met before? Perhaps he was a friend of my father? Or was this destiny at work, something illusive, mystical, spiritual? I could think of no rational explanation for this passing confusion but knew on some intangible level there was a bond, a special reason why Charlie Rolfe had walked into the office that afternoon and why we were together in the entrance hall of Black Spires.

He took a camera from his bag and took photographs as we made our way through the house, but I got the feeling that Charlie Rolfe wasn't really looking at anything. He was looking at me. In my short skirt I was conscious that after climbing the stairs with him and passing through the bedrooms, sweat was sticky on my back and the flush felt like fire on my neck and throat.

After going downstairs, Charlie suggested we go up again. He let me lead the way. We stood in the back bedroom overlooking the long garden with its apple and pear trees. He took some shots through the window, then asked me to pose on one side of the frame. I knew that shooting into the light produced awful pictures, but he set up a laptop on a small table, linked it with a long cord, and when he showed me the images I appeared with an intense but oddly elated expression, my body a silhouette surrounded by an aura of pale-blue light. It was stunning: I looked like a different person, and when I looked back at Charlie Rolfe I realised I was panting for breath.

The sun had come out from behind a cloud and the light in the room was both hazy and dazzling like light through water. I remembered learning in some long-distant art class that in photography time does not exist except as a series of frozen moments managed by some higher form of physics in which the person and the photograph are separated, not by time, but imagination.

'Can I take another couple of shots?'

''Course,' I gushed and, although I knew he was talking about taking shots of me, I had processed the question as if he wanted to take more shots of the room.

He set up a video camera on a tripod. He spent a long time adjusting the lens, but then approached with his digital camera. He told me to stand at the side of the window with the sun lighting just one side of my face. The camera clicked and he changed angle. I suppose I had seen models in magazines and on TV and you sort of know how to act, how to pose. As Charlie Rolfe moved around the room, I changed positions, jutting out my hips, turning to peer over one shoulder with expressions that were arrogant, alluring, provocative. The click, click, click of the camera was like a metronome beating out the rhythm and lulling me into a sense of . . . a sense of what I'm not sure, but when he asked me to pull my blouse off one shoulder, I didn't hesitate: I was living in the moment and wanted to be and do and feel everything that had always been risqué, out of touch, too old for me. After all the exams, the confines of boarding school, I wanted to taste life. Lots of confused feelings were rushing around my head as the camera kept clicking and Charlie's soft dark voice encouraged me.

'More. More. That's it. That's lovely, that's perfect,' he was saying. 'Milly, undo another button on your blouse, it'll look nice.'

And I undid another button, leaning forward to reveal my sun-browned breasts like a model in a magazine.

6

'I am going to buy this house, Milly,' he said.

'Really?'

A bead of perspiration ran down my back. If he bought the house I'd get thousands of pounds in commission, my university fees paid in one sweep of luck. I didn't know what to do with my hands and when I gripped them behind my back, I realised I was pushing out my breasts. He stared into my eyes.

'Milly, will you do something for me?'

He didn't say what. He just looked at me and I nodded.

'Of course,' I said.

'Take your top off for me.'

The words came from his mouth like a coil of silver smoke and seemed to hang there like a bubble.

Take your top off for me.

It was such a simple sentence. Such a simple request. My tingling nipples were tingling even more. I wanted to release them, give them air. The trickle of sweat on my back turned cold and made me shiver. The silence stretched. I was a rabbit caught in the headlights of his sapphire eyes, immobile, terrified, excited.

'Take your top off for me.'

He said it again, his velvety voice deeper and darker like the words were no longer a wisp of smoke but words whispered from far away. They reached me like a recording that had been slowed down.

Take your top off for me.

Just as I often knew what my mother was going to say before she said it, I had known Charlie Rolfe was going to ask me to take off my top, but the *for me* tagged onto the sentence was puzzling, and the politeness of the request made it difficult to say no without seeming disrespectful. I felt flustered, embarrassed. And I felt energised, too. I had willed this. I must have known something was in the air when I removed my bra that morning. I had been thinking wanton thoughts and he had read my mind. Was it too late to stop?

'I can't do that,' I finally mumbled.

'Milly?' He waited.

'Yes.'

'I won't tell you again.'

'But . . .'

He took a deep breath. I sensed rather than saw the faint shake of his head. The disappointment. I was no more than an overgrown schoolgirl with my head full of cheap fantasies, a pathetic little virgin. I had failed. I would never sell Black Spires. I wouldn't get a place at Durham or St Andrews or Cambridge. I was doomed.

'Please,' I said, but my will had gone.

He raised his brow, the upward motion acting as a spring that resonated from his blue eyes to my arms. It was quite uncanny, a stage trick, an electric pulse, a radio wave. As his brow went up and his eyes flashed, I wriggled my right arm out of the narrow sleeve, raised the cotton blouse over my hair and ran the material down my left arm to my hand. I realised I had been holding my breath and let out a long sigh. We stood there in the silvery light, my breasts standing out firm and full, my nipples hard and painful, pink and shiny with a rush of blood.

He took several pictures, but they weren't very good. I wasn't posing, just standing there. He clicked his fingers and pointed.

'If you please.'

I went to speak but my mouth just fell open and nothing came out. My breasts were already on show, sun-bronzed and pretty, throbbing with the beat of my heart. Breasts are everywhere. In every newspaper and magazine, at bus stops and on television. But my skirt? The thought whizzed through my brain like an elec-

8

tronic pulse, but even as I determined to shake my head and say no, I reached for the snap and lowered the zip.

I wriggled my hips and my breasts faintly swayed as the skirt fell in a pink pool about my feet. It was warm in that sunny room, perspiration veneered the split in my bottom and my knickers were damp where I had leaked in the gusset. I could smell the faint perfume of my own arousal and realised with shame that the obscure pleasure of that moment came not from any expectation of what might take place, but simply from exposing myself.

'Very good,' he said.

My pink knickers fitted snugly, the elastic stretching like a bridge from the supports of my hip bones in such a way that, had Mr Rolfe leaned forward, he would have got a glimpse of the dark little forest of hair nestling below.

He adjusted the camera.

'Those, too,' he said.

His voice was a chant, whispering my own inner desires. Each time he asked for more, I gave more, my blouse, my skirt. I was on a slippery slide. There was no way off. I didn't want to get off. I slid my thumbs into the sides of my panties, drew them over my hips, revealing the dark crease of my bottom, over the round cheeks that he said were so pretty and down my long legs. I was naked. I was free. I felt alive. Completely and totally alive. I spread my legs and leaned over the polished surface of the narrow table between the two tall arched windows. The camera clicked and captured my most intimate parts, my moist pussy, the hole in my bottom.

'That's lovely. Nice. Very nice. Lean over the table, Milly. Come on now, push out that bottom. Nice. Nice. Give it to me. Give me more.'

I slipped out of my shoes and climbed onto the table. He didn't need to tell me how to arrange myself, you just know these things: on my hands and knees with my bottom pushed out, my breasts hanging like two warm heavy udders. I wiggled like a pony and the more I wiggled the more the camera clicked and the wetter I got. I was drenched. I could feel contractions inside me and I just wanted to touch myself.

'Lay back, Milly, legs up, that's nice. That's nice.'

He was reading my mind. I spread my legs and my palms with stretched fingers went automatically to my breasts. The teats were brilliant-red and on fire. I turned the little buds and squealed in pain and the pain turned to pleasure. I ran my right hand down my side, across the bony curve of my hip and into my pubic hair. My pubes were drenched. I could smell sex in the air and as I slid my fingers inside my wet crack it was such a relief. I nursed my clitoris, teasing it like a cat with a toy mouse. The juices gushed from me, hot and sticky, and the camera was clicking away. I threw my head back, and through my orgasm I rose clean off the table and would have fallen I'm sure had Charlie not lifted me in his arms.

He carried me to the bed. I was gasping, rocking back and forth, a sea of hot liquid bursting from me in a tide and coating my thighs. Nothing like this had ever happened before. I had masturbated, lots and lots of times, but the film stars and rock stars that fuelled my fantasy were an illusion and Charlie Rolfe was real and had touched something in me that had been waiting anxiously to be touched.

He turned the video lens to face the bed. I wasn't watching him, I was drawn to the eye of the camera, mesmerised by its ability to capture this moment. The preposterous thing was that at eighteen I had never

10

allowed any of the boys I had met on school holidays to go all the way. I was a virgin still and this implausible state was about to be recorded as it came to an end. There was doubt and confusion in my head, fear too, and I knew I would think about it all later, I would remember always, but for now I lay back on the bed cover and watched Charlie Rolfe remove his denim shirt, his jeans, his boxers, I watched his long hard cock spring to attention, and I arched my legs to allow him to enter my body.

There was no ceremony, no kissing, no foreplay. I was sopping and he entered me immediately, pushing hard and jerking upwards at the same time. The rush of pain as my hymen snapped brought a tear to my eye and I thought about the camera, how it would preserve that instant, that small tear, the look of pain and pleasure that spread over my greedy features as I pulled him up inside me, filling me, completing me, the light crossing the room and turning slowly to shadow.

Charlie Rolfe never did buy Black Spires. I dropped him off at the station and I never saw him again – although that's not strictly true. I have seen his naked back and white bottom many times. The video he shot found its way onto the internet and if you search the deep dark recesses of the web you can watch me losing my virginity over and over again.

– Milly, Kent, UK

My Lady's Chamber

The smell and feel of other people's houses. I love it. The silence when the front door slams and they leave you there alone. Treading over lush carpet or cool floorboards. Exploring. Touching smooth banisters, embossed wallpaper, flowers. Turning their taps. Playing their music. Slurping their Pouilly Fumé from the fridge.

Kitchens have the character. Bedrooms have the mystery. If it's the other way round there's something weird. But the more posh the house, the less the rooms will give away. Why? One word. Staff. Someone's taking care of everything. That's why it's spotless. That's why you won't see the evidence.

Bedrooms are my favourite. Especially when they're still dark, musty, with drawn curtains, hopelessly untidy. So warm you can smell the breath. You always catch them out in the end if you come and go for long enough. If you become part of the furniture. Part of the household, really.

Beds all rumpled from sleep or fighting or steaming rampant sex. The stains and marks on them, and I'm not talking about red wine or coffee. I mean body stains. Juices. Semen and sweat. Those intimate messes draw me. I can't help it. I want to get right in there, it's like

I want to find something really dirty. Most of all, I want to smell it. It arouses me, makes me hot, whatever, I'm excited and appalled at the same time.

I'll never forget the first time I entered someone's bedroom and saw the sheet stuck into a kind of stiff pale ridge where the guy had come some time in the night. And a few spots of dried blood. You go right into their souls. They'd given me a key and everything and were *letting me in.*

I always take my time in a new house before I allow myself the ultimate pleasure of opening the bedroom door. Actually I take my time even if it's a familiar place. Each time I arrive I'll spot something new. I force myself to walk around, dawdle on the stairs, poke round the other rooms first. Then I'm in there. The master bedroom. The houses I go to all have master bedrooms. I don't work anywhere cheap. The effect on me is the same every time. The first thing I do is crawl over the bed, on hands and knees, even with my shoes on, like to leave my own dirt, then I lie down, get right in and under, sniff the sheets and pillows and those damp pale stains.

And then there's the clothes. Without the right staff there's always clothes draped and dropped over the bed, the chair, mostly the floor, knickers tangled up maybe with cashmere sweaters or a man's jacket. I pick them up, all the clothes, and press them into my face to sniff them. Yes, especially the knickers.

Jewellery. They always have jewellery in the bedroom, gold and diamonds jumbled up with hairbrushes and books and bottles of ever-beautifying anti-ageing lotion and topless lipsticks and shredded bits of cotton wool. And as every burglar knows, up there is where the cash will be, and the passports, and any other piece of vital expensive information. Funny that people keep all their valuables in the same obvious room. Their whole life is stashed or tidied or spilled around them, while they sleep.

No, I'm not a burglar! Though I can see why you thought that. And I could tell everything a burglar needed to know if he wanted to break into a house like this one. And I'm not always scrupulously honest. They leave me alone here, you see, so trusting. I've nicked things, of course I have. But I call it a bonus. A tip. And they're so grateful for everything they never say a word.

But this house is the best yet. Don't you think it's gorgeous! Spotless? Of course it is. That's all down to me. I'm their cleaner. Didn't you realise? It's because I'm not wearing my overall today. That's the other thing I love about this job. The uniform. My choice, but the employers all think it's great. Maybe because while it makes me look submissive, it makes them feel superior. It's short, Persil-white, button-through. That marks me out as staff, you see. No messing.

Anyway, this house is the best of all the houses I clean. I take great pride in doing it just how Sophia likes it. If I wasn't planning to move on I'd want to work here forever. I so want to please her. Especially now I've seen what she's like when she's naked.

'Slovenly is a dirty word, Josephine,' she told me on my first day here. 'It goes with slut.'

She was standing at the top of the stairs, snapping shut a powder-blue briefcase. She was framed by the light from the landing window. You can see all the dust motes dancing when it's a hot day. I was at the bottom of the stairs, holding a can of Pledge.

'I want this house so clean you could lick it.'

I could see straight up her skirt. Incredibly slim thighs, slightly parted, twitching with impatient muscles. At the top of her leg just the corner, the curve, of one plump sex lip. Either no knickers, or the tiniest thong. Quite shocking, unexpected, to see.

'Even the floors, Mrs Palmer?'

'Call me Sophia. Though we won't have much time to chat. I travel a lot.'

She has a slightly foreign accent. Polish? That's Polish from Poland, not polish like Pledge. She smiled at me, doing up a button in the centre of her cleavage. 'Yes, even the floors. Sometimes I might test them to see how clean they are. When you least expect me.'

'You'll get down on all fours to lick the floors, Sophia?'

'No, Josephine.' She came down the stairs and I could smell her heavy perfume. She stalked straight past me and picked up her car keys. 'You will.'

'She's so uptight, it's not true,' grumbled my predecessor later that morning as she climbed onto her motorbike. 'You're welcome to her.' Having shown me the ropes she was off interviewing for a housekeeper's job for some rock star or other. 'Christ, the way she dresses, the way she talks, she makes Margaret Thatcher look like Pamela Anderson.'

I fingered the silk knickers I'd taken from the wash basket and hidden in my pocket. I was thinking of Sophia on all fours, licking the parquet. 'I think pussy bows are sexy.'

'Pussies, yes.' The woman stared at my cute uniform, ran her tongue over her lips. It occurred to me that she might be a dyke. 'Those pert little secretary blouses, no.'

'Well, I think she's beautiful, like Grace Kelly. Like a princess.' *And those pert little blouses always show the nipples. The silk slides cold against them, making them harden and poke through . . .* 'I wish she was here every day.'

'Ice queen more like.' The bike belched out blue smoke. Sophia's previous cleaner swung her leather-clad leg over the saddle. 'Travelling the world, earning a fortune. But she'll love you with your plaits and your pinny. You're her mini-me, after all.' She meant it as an insult, but I was thrilled with that. Her mini-me. 'But you'll want to watch him. It has to be perfect. Gerald's a towel straightener.'

Did I mention other people's bathrooms? You wouldn't think they were sexy, would you, not like those dishevelled bedrooms. There's the potential for dirt in bathrooms, isn't there? Human dirt. What Sophia would call slovenly. Slutty. Yet the bathroom is where Gerald keeps the towels straight, the soap and bottles in rigid rows, as if he wants to deny all the washing and shitting that goes on in there.

I stayed out of their bathroom for the first week. Concentrated on cleaning the reception rooms downstairs. She hadn't returned from her travels, as far as I knew. The second week I walked through the master bedroom into the huge en-suite to look for signs of her. I squatted down to sniff the towels, careful not to move them. They smelt of very strong, expensive soap. I was about to pull away when I caught a tang of something female and arousing.

I sniffed again, pulling the towel off the rail. Sophia had forbidden me to do the laundry. So the towels hadn't been washed since she went away. I got wet imagining her rubbing the towel between her legs. I hitched my tight overall up over my hips and dabbed at my knickers with the towel. I was already so damp. She would wipe her pussy, maybe open it a little to pat it dry, make herself wet all over again when the towel snagged on her clit. She'd be wet this time with pussy juice not water.

16

I leaned back against the loo seat, dizzy with lust, and dragged the towel quickly over my cunt, imagining her frisking herself, rubbing those tender pink bits till she was sore. I rubbed the towel over my knickers, pushing the wet fabric up so it sliced into my crack, rubbed harder as I thought of her head falling back, her hair spilling over the loo seat, her mouth opening to moan out loud.

Just at that moment I caught sight of a blonde woman sprawled on the floor with her legs open, towel whipping up and down, and realised the whole wall of the bathroom was mirrored, and it was me. Sophia's mini-me. That made me come. I watched myself, seeing Sophia, and came, surrounded by her soap and potions, bucking against the floor, grinding against the towel. I'd never watched myself before, but I wanted to do it and I wanted to come just like she would.

I never thought of myself as a lesbian. I still don't think I am. It's just that she's so beautiful. It's like a schoolgirl crush. Overwhelming. Enough to excite me. If I'm honest, I've been in a perpetual state of excitement from the moment I stepped into this house. All the cleaning, polishing, hoovering, wiping. Upstairs, downstairs, in my lady's chamber, it all led to her. So it was natural to want to be in her most private of rooms, masturbating against her towel, thinking about her face, her cunt, while I was coming.

The next week I lingered downstairs in the study, because there were leather-bound books, ornaments and trophies to polish. And because I found some photographs in the desk, blown-up black and whites of Sophia posing on a beach here, on the lawn there, leaning against a tree in a spooky forest, all tastefully composed, naked or wearing a bikini or with diaphanous veils draped round her. She looked like a model.

I took a couple of them home with me and got my brother to scan them. Just before it was time to pack up on the Friday, I went up to the bedroom. Immaculate. No need that day to tidy or clean it. I wandered over to her dressing table and saw amongst the glass bottles a hairbrush. Not a single gold hair. And tossed in an empty crystal vase, a diamond ring, so enormous it could have come out of a cracker. I picked it up and looked around. Sometimes in that house I felt like I was being watched. I *wanted* to be watched, actually. I'm not so weird I want to be alone *all* the time. If you're not messing around with things or playing with yourself it can get dull. I put the ring on my finger and then went into the bathroom.

This time the towels had been changed. They smelt of detergent. Again they were hung in exact rows. I'd promised myself this treat. It felt so good last time, rubbing myself with her things. But this time I couldn't smell her. It was all too clean. I sat on the loo and started to rub at myself. Half-heartedly at first, but I was excited again in no time. All I had to do was listen to the silence of the house and think of Sophia. Then I wanted to wee. I'd been playing a little game all day, deliberately forbidding myself from cleaning or even entering the bedroom suite until the end of my shift. But I'd had too much coffee in their kitchen. Too much spring water and a little wine in their drawing room. The pricking in my bladder was too urgent.

As I straddled the loo I caught sight of myself again. Overall hitched up, tight over my hips, white knickers down round my knees, thighs bulging on the loo seat. My legs pressed together. I opened them slowly, saw the plump lips stuck together, joined under a soft line of hair. My bladder was loosening now. I stuck my fingers down, staring at myself in the mirror all the while, and

18

parted those lips, felt the stickiness inside and the lovely warmth. There was the first delicious sting of the first trickle.

Earlier that day I'd put my hair up in a chignon, just like a photograph of Sophia I'd seen downstairs. So prim. So dirty. A slut, pissing in her lady's chamber! What would she say? I'd tell her that slut was a dirty word, but in a good way. I'd show her how, make her put her hand where my fingers were, pulling my lips open, make her feel the first hot drops, and as I rehearsed our conversation I let another couple more seep out, elongating through the curls of hair, hanging there. I shivered, waiting for the pale yellow stream to start, knowing what a relief it would be, like a climax pouring through me, wishing, oh God, wishing Sophia was there to see. Her face pushed up near my legs, maybe, kneeling there like a golden saint, watching me pee, watching like we used to peep at the older girls at school. She'd be telling me I was dirty, but her face would be too close and it would spray on her, and I'd lift my hips over her beautiful face and piss all over it –

I couldn't hold on. I let out a little moan as I let it run through my fingers, stinging on the inside of my thighs. Her mouth with its perfect smearing of red lipstick would open, tongue stuck out to lap at it, she'd drink the neat yellow jet –

The wee pricked my skin. I heard a phone ring in the bedroom, echoed in jangling bells through the house. I jumped up, wiped myself dry with the towel, and hung it exactly in the middle of the other two towels, wet patch in.

Sophia still hadn't returned by the third week. By now I'd cleaned the house from top to bottom, and seen no one. Only the old gardener, occasionally. I knew that

Mr Palmer had been home because the post I laid out for him on the hall table was always gone.

Haven't I mentioned Gerald?

Gerald caught me, in the end.

You see, that house in Hampstead started to feel like my own. I didn't sleep there – well, only the occasional afternoon nap – but I started to do extra days just so I could explore some more, and he always left out the right cash for me. As if he knew when I was there. What hours I did. Anyway, the day he caught me I suppose I'd gone too far. I didn't even bother giving downstairs the once-over. How many times can you flick a duster over an empty fireplace, for God's sake?

I went straight upstairs to the bedroom. I was feeling really cavalier that day, really feisty, because I took a big glass of wine up with me, glugging as I went, just as if I was the lady of the house. I was just about to walk through to the bathroom with my glass of wine, my pussy already clenching with excitement at the thought of which towels would be there, how straight, the mirror, how it would feel when I started to rub myself against them, when something in the bedroom stopped me. Something was different. For a start, it smelt different. I stood by the bed like some bloody greyhound, sniffing the air and walked over to the French window, still sniffing. So subtle it could have been a single flower, or the armpit of a man's shirt.

It could have been an open pot of cream on the dressing table giving off that smell. But there was only a single white rose there, very fresh, and it had no scent. I checked in the mirror that my hair was done as she would do it. This time in a French pleat. In the mirror I saw that the bed was turned back. Like in a hotel. Just the corner, turned back. It looked so inviting. I lay down. Stretched myself out. It was a hot day. I

20

unbuttoned my overall, threw it to the floor, then stretched out again, my bare limbs writhing all over the smooth Egyptian cotton. My head swam a little from the wine. I rubbed my nose deep into the sheet, searching for that elusive scent.

I rolled over a few times, stretching, pretending I was Sophia waking up after an afternoon nap. But if I was Sophia I'd be wearing her clothes, right? I crawled across the soft white carpet. I knew exactly where she kept her underwear. Folded in long flat drawers in a pretty Art Deco chest of drawers. I pulled out some pale-pink French knickers, kicked off my own, slid the cool silk of hers up my legs, let the silk embrace my pussy and catch a little in the crack of my buttocks as I danced about in her bedroom.

And underneath the knickers, a neat stack of DVDs. No labels. I pushed one quickly into the little silver TV concealed behind an Impressionist painting. No title. No intro. No credits. Just a woman, naked, on all fours, licking the floor. Her bottom was towards the camera and, as she crawled forwards to lick the floor, her cheeks parted, showing the long dark crease. There was no sound, maybe some soft music in the background. I recognised the black and white diamond tiles of the hall floor. The woman lifted her head as if obeying instructions, as if she knew I was watching her, and of course it was Sophia.

She glanced over her shoulder, her mouth curling in a smile, total coquette, then she bent to lick the floor again, sticking her bottom right up in the air, and this time her fingers appeared between her buttocks, spreading them further open and now I could see the pink slit of her cunt too, and her ring finger was poking in and out of it, wearing the exact same diamond that I had just tried on, and Christ now my golden Sophia was stretching her thumb to nudge it into the little purple pucker hole of her arse.

The camera zoomed in on that, on her thumb, urging the hole open like a petal. Her nail went inside, and the hole closed round it like a tight mouth. The film paused there, froze the frame, enough to make me realise that my hand was shoved down the knickers, my own fingers exploring the warm crack of my bottom just like Sophia. Except that I didn't quite dare. I didn't dare go that far, stick my finger up my shit hole, for all my talk of liking it dirty.

Then the film cut, as if they knew I'd be watching. I was kneeling on the bed now, my fingers being sucked in by my cunt. I stared at the television, almost whimpering with frustration, then suddenly the film started again, but in quicker motion now, cutting brutally back and forth. There was a close-up of Sophia, lying just where I was on the bed, staring straight at me, her mouth red and glistening with lipstick, open like I'd imagined her drinking my piss, and then a huge cock came into shot and slid straight into her mouth. The film speeded up, cutting to other brief shots of her breasts, with other hands stroking them, a tongue licking the hard nipples, then another shot of a cock thrusting in and out of a white, waxed pussy, then again her mouth sucking on that big cock, another shot of her thumb, right up her arse now, mouth sucking the big cock again, the nipples, then her face, looking over her shoulder, her mouth opening, smiling, and Sophia crooning, faster and louder, 'Ooh, fuck me!'

'Oh, fuck me!' I echoed, getting up on my knees, watching the television, panting as the shots speeded up, letting my nipples rub against the duvet, my fingers rubbing quicker up and down my cunt, imitating her, wishing I was her, wriggling my arse about in her

French knickers as my own fingers slid into me. Now she was moaning something else. His name.

'Gerry, Gerry,' I moaned back, pushing my fingers as far inside as they would go, feeling my cunt closing round them, the first clenching ripple of nearby orgasm –

'Gerald to you.'

A pair of big hands clamped down on my hips, dragging me backwards across the bed. I squealed. My fingers slipped out of my pussy as I scrabbled at the duvet, releasing the scent of my excitement. In the dressing-table mirror I could see, behind me, a man with dark hair. I knelt up, tried to twist round, but he tangled his fingers in my hair to keep me still and facing forwards.

'Who's been sleeping in my bed?' his deep voice demanded. He tugged at my hair, jerked my head backwards. I love my hair being touched. Even roughly like that. 'Fucking Goldilocks?'

On the TV screen my goddess Sophia was being fucked on this very bed. Her blonde head banged rhythmically, violently, against the headboard. Her nipples poked up in the air, rigid and red, so you knew she was enjoying it. All you could see of the man fucking her was the muscular bulge of his bare arm then, as the camera panned round, his buttocks, banging at her, his balls swinging under him like some great bullock's, then gradually shrinking as the fucking got harder. A shot of his thick hard cock going in.

'It's only me, Mr Palmer, Josephine.' My voice came out as a breathy whisper. 'I'm very sorry. I shouldn't have touched your things –'

He was close up behind me. He was dressed. I saw his wrists, in snowy white French cuffs, cufflinks. A signet ring. The hand with the signet ring jabbed a remote control at the television, and Sophia's face was snuffed out. I wanted her back.

23

'I know it's you, Josie.' He pushed me back down in front of him, letting my hair swing round my face, and I could hear the swift tearing of his zip. He kicked a leg, or knee, between my thighs, opening them up. 'I know you've been touching my things, Josie. Sophia's things. You've been making them dirty. Look.'

There was a shot of the study. Then there was me, laying out those photographs on the desk. Bending down to kiss the pictures of Sophia.

'I'm sorry, Gerald. It's only because I think she's so beautiful.'

'And so are you, Josie. You look like her, did you know?'

This time the camera lingered on the top of a blonde head, the hair in a French plait. A sharp cheekbone. Eyelashes. The camera trailed down, and it was me sitting on their en-suite loo, my thighs open. The camera was steady, focusing on my hand, moving over my pussy, then on the messy spray of piss settling into a thin arc, golden yellow, jetting into the pan.

'I'm sorry, Gerald. I didn't mean –'

But the sight of it made me hot. After I'd finished pissing, after I'd wiped myself on the towel, the camera paused on my hand, wet with a few drops of piss, wearing the diamond ring.

'Sorry doesn't cover it. You're a little thief, as well as a prowler!'

'I'll give the ring back. I was only trying it on. I'm here to clean, Gerald.'

'And I'm here to give you orders.' He grabbed my hand, fingers still sticky with my juice, twisted it behind me. My fingers closed round his big warm cock and he moved my hand up and down the shaft. It got harder, and bigger. I wanted it inside me. The room was shadowy now. I couldn't see Gerald clearly in the reflection.

'Let's watch the home movie again. Goldilocks, pissing in my loo. You see, I'm tidy, but I don't want everything so clean. It's Sophia who wants everything scrubbed. That's why I have to fuck her till she gets all messed up. I fuck her till she's a dirty little slut again, like you. Oh, she hates me for it.'

The film looped round again. There was Sophia, stripped. Her hair, falling out of its pins. Her beautiful cool face distorting into ecstasy, body bucking like a porn star's. She writhed on the screen in front of me while I massaged her husband's cock and watched his hands in the mirror, pinching my nipples.

God, that made me horny. I was like a bitch on heat. I'd had weeks of wandering round this stunning house, making myself at home, helping myself to little things they wouldn't miss. A few crisp tenners here, a diamond trinket there. Every time something went in my pocket, even if it was just a sock, I got horny. Weeks of fantasising, playing with myself, wanting Sophia, while what I really needed was a good fucking. And I was about to get it. Even better – I was about to get it from the master of the house.

'Are you going to fuck me, Gerald?' It came out as a kind of pathetic mewing. I liked the sound. Made me the wee wench. I pushed my bottom against his cock, angled it up between my cheeks.

'I'm going to punish you, greedy little bitch.'

My mouth on the screen, and in the mirror, was open. My tongue was flicking across my wet lips as I spread my legs open with my fingers and started, in the film, to piss. In the mirror my tits dangled into my master's hands. I pulled harder at his cock and started to rock against him.

His cock was massive in my hands. I knew he wouldn't be able to pull away now. My butt cheeks closed round it. His balls nudged my clit. He was groaning in my ear now, as his wife groaned on the screen, and my legs started to melt apart.

I tried to inch his knob inside me but he bent me forwards so I lost my grip on him and dropped onto my hands. My pussy was dripping with excitement now and all I could do was watch my shadowy lover as he released my tits, let the sore nipples brush against the duvet.

At last he hooked my – sorry, his wife's – French knickers down my legs and cupped my wet bush. One long finger went straight into my wet crack, just where my own fingers had been but how much better someone else's finger felt. My master's finger in my lady's chamber. A cold cufflink caught on my skin. I squealed. He pushed me down roughly, started to circle my wet pussy lips, shoved two more fingers up me.

My face was stuffed into the duvet now, my bottom up in the air. And now Gerald's cock was pushing into the crevice of my bottom. I reached up to cup the balls dangling beneath his cock and they retracted slightly at my touch.

'Let's see how dirty you can be, Josie.'

His knob was pushing at my arse hole.

'No, don't put it in there.'

I tried to shift sideways, direct his knob down to my cunt, but he dragged my hips up towards him. His fingers were hooked into my cunt to keep me in place. One of his fingertips tweaked my clit. My cunt was going into a spasm. But now his cock was nudging into my hole, pushing hard against the tight ring trying to repel him. Then it slipped in and Gerald gave a great sigh.

'What trouble you'll be in now, when she sees this on the DVD,' he said. 'Filthy enough, do you think?'

I moaned, unable to speak, impaled on his fingers and his cock, helpless. All my thoughts were centred on what he was doing to me. I gave up trying to see his reflection clearly, to make out his features. But actually, who cared about his face? He was inside me now. His cock was up my arse, and my arse was loosening to let him further in. It felt slippery, and strange. It felt so good.

But then something caught my eye in the glass. A movement. It wasn't him, and it wasn't me.

'Stop!' I squeaked. 'Look!'

'Stop?' he muttered, starting deliberately, slowly, to slide himself up me, pushing my face back into the duvet. 'You must be bloody joking.'

Someone standing in the doorway, reflected in the mirror. My shock turned to wicked excitement. Someone dressed in a white suit, holding a powder-blue briefcase. If Gerald saw her, he didn't care. He didn't alter his rhythm. And I didn't want him to. Sophia standing there was like an electric probe, and I started to gyrate frantically. I wanted her to see her husband ramming me hard up the backside.

'Dirty, isn't she? Taking it up the arse, where it's so dirty.'

Gerald's voice came out in grunts now.

Sophia didn't speak. She came into the room, dropped the briefcase on the bed. Came and stood in front of me, right in front of my face. Gerald fucked me harder, rocking me towards her. My body was straining to keep hold of him, straining to keep the flood of orgasm at bay.

'This is how I'm rewarded after a tough trip?' Sophia tipped my chin so that I was staring at her. 'My husband screwing the little slut? Up her dirty little bottom? Now we'll have to make everything clean again. I'm so disappointed, Josephine.'

27

I couldn't speak. I was about to come. Gerald's cock was speeding up, he was about to come, he was going to come up inside my arse and his fingers were playing across my clit, shoving roughly up my cunt.

Gerald's cock pushed on up me until it could go no further. I slid down onto him until I could go no further. And then he held my hips totally still, forcing us both to pause again.

'So do what she says, Josie,' he murmured. I moaned and bucked with frustration.

'Apologise?' I croaked, my muscles twitching and gripping at him, my arms shaking with the effort of holding myself up.

Sophia knelt on the bed just in front of me, lifted up her skirt and pushed her white, waxed pussy, split by its sliver of silver thong, into my face.

'No, Josephine. Lick me. I'm tired and dirty and sweaty after my trip. Lick me clean.'

Her sex lips squashed into my face, opening to reveal her red clit. Gerald started thrusting violently, ramming full-length inside my tight anus, nearly lifting me off my knees with the force of his thrusting.

That smell, from the towel, was thick in my nostrils. Sophia took hold of my hair and pushed my face harder against her, opening her lips with her other hand. Gerald jerked faster and faster at me and my pussy got tighter as my orgasm crashed over me. I stuck my tongue out and licked up her crack, tasted her sweat and piss and sweet juices, and licked again.

I came and shrieked and moaned against my lady's chamber, licking at her wet slit like a cat, licking her clean. Gerald snatched his fingers out of me and gripped my hips until he'd finished thrusting and coming. His cock stayed stiff, gripped inside me as I licked at Sophia, her fingers pulling my hair, banging my teeth and nose

28

and tongue against her, and she came quickly, grinding herself against my face and then falling onto the bed beside me. Gerald pulled out of me and I crumpled in a heap between them, juice running down my thighs.

Did they give me the sack? After that kind of home movie? You must be joking! Did I have to lick the floor? Yes, and still do. Frequently, when they get home from work and the house isn't done to perfection.

Like I said, I'll move on. But not just yet.

– *Josie, Kensington, UK*

Louise

I always thought of myself as a regular guy, until I met Louise. It started out as an ordinary date. A mate of mine was going out with this girl called Cathy, and Louise was staying with Cathy. I came along to see *Get Carter* with them, just so Louise wouldn't feel like a gooseberry, and we hit it off. After a couple of dates we got together, like you do, back at my flat one night after a Chinese and maybe one too many Tiger beers.

It was a good night, but there was nothing weird. She left the light on, which I like, and wanted to go on top, which I don't mind, especially if the girl has decent-sized tits, because the way they jiggle up and down as she rides just drives me wild. Louise had good tits, not big so much, but a handful each, and firm. She had a good body all round, as it goes, slim but not really skinny, with long legs and a little round arse so firm you could have parked a push-bike between her cheeks. To look at her face, and the way she dressed, with long brown hair pinned up and a skirt-suit she wore for work, you'd think she was your average girl. She wasn't, not by a long way.

We did the normal thing, I suppose, going out together a few times, starting to sleep together, then moving in together. At first it was really hot, sex all the time, and not just in the bedroom but in the living room, the kitchen, the bathroom, anywhere, we were at it like rabbits. All that was great, and even when the sex started to cool off we got on well, so we decided to try and spice it up a bit. You know the stuff, dressing up and a bit of bondage, only it didn't really do it for me, not until one night when we'd come back from the pub and were messing about in the living room.

She'd started to strip off for me, which I've always been well into, dancing nice and slow as she peeled off her clothes, and extra sexy 'cause she was in her office suit. I love to see a smart girl get naked, it's so much hornier than if she's dressed for sex from the off, especially Louise, 'cause she would go from looking real prim and proper to sex on legs.

Normally she'd go all the way, stark naked, by which time I'd be well ready for her and she'd climb on my lap the way she liked it. This time she went down to her undies – knickers, bra, a pair of stockings – and the shiny black heels she wore at the office. After that, I usually got a peep show, tits first, teasing me by pulling her bra cups up and down, then bum, stuck out while she took her knickers down nice and slow. This time she went back to dancing, still holding her skirt and using it to tease me with, hiding herself and then pulling it away just as she turned around. I was rock hard, and I would have grabbed her, only she suddenly throws her skirt at me, right over my cock, and I remember what she said as if it was yesterday.

'Put it on. Go on, put my skirt on, or I won't go any further.'

The state I was in, I'd have dressed up like Ronald McDonald if she'd asked me to, and I've always been up for a laugh. So I stripped off, double-quick, and pulled her skirt on up my legs, and all the while she's standing there watching me with her hands on her hips.

She had this real intense look on her face, and she wasn't laughing at me like I'd expected, just staring.

Of course the skirt didn't fit, but I managed to get it up with the zip undone and I turned it around so that didn't show and there I was, in a woman's skirt, only with my cock sticking up at the front like a flagpole. It felt really weird, but I can't deny it was a turn-on, like I'd done something a bit naughty, and like I was exposed in a way that said I was ready for sex, only not in the way I'm used to. It's hard to describe, but what I do know is that my cock felt like a steel rod, and Louise was well into it.

She called me a good boy, which turned me on even more, like I knew I could do anything in front of her, or anything with her. I sat down again, and pulled the skirt up a bit to get at my cock as she went back to dancing, slow and sexy as she started to give me my peep show. How I didn't burst I do not know, because she was so good, better than ever before, and so turned on I could see the wet at the front of her panties. By the time she kicked them off she was moaning, and she climbed straight on, taking hold of me and guiding me in up her cunt.

As she rode me she kept touching where the skirt was pulled tight around my hips and tugging the hem up and down my legs, like she couldn't get enough of me being in it. When she came it was like an explosion, rubbing herself on me and gasping and screaming, just like a porn star, only for real. I was a bit shocked, to tell the truth, 'cause I'd never seen her so horny. That didn't stop me coming. It was like she was sucking me dry, and I could feel the tightness of her skirt on my hips as I did it, like that was the most exciting thing.

I felt a bit odd about it after that first time, like it made me gay or something. Only how could I be gay?

Louise was all woman, and just because I'd got off on wearing her skirt didn't mean I wanted a bloke instead. She was well into it too, relaxed and excited all at once, like she was welcoming me into a part of herself she'd never shown before. I'd had my fair share of relationships before, good and bad, but this was different, more intimate.

It didn't happen for a bit after that first time, until one night when we'd come back from a fancy-dress party. She'd gone as a sexy pirate, with this short skirt, in red, with lots of layers. The waist was elastic, and on the way home she was joking that it would fit me and that I should put it on when we got home. I kept thinking how nice it had felt with my cock hard under a little skirt and by the time we got in I was well ready.

She made me strip off in the hall, all the way to nude, and she gave me the skirt. It felt so good, just pulling it up my legs, and once it was on I got that same feeling, of being able to let myself go completely. She was loving it, just like before, and she made me show off for her, like she used to for me, like I was the girl. I got hard doing it, I couldn't help myself, so my cock was sticking up under the hem of the skirt. She loved that, and took me in her hand, telling me I was a bad boy, and that she was going to wank me off just so I didn't have a hard-on any more. Her hand had gone up the back of my skirt, and as she wanked me she began to slap at my bottom, like she was punishing me for getting a hard-on.

It felt weird, and I was a bit ashamed of myself, but it felt too good for me to want to stop it, especially when she was having so much fun. She kept touching the skirt, like she needed to feel it as well as me, and all the while slapping at my bottom and wanking my prick. I came all over her hand, and the skirt, I couldn't help it. Then she did something else, just as horny.

First she made me suck what I'd done off her fingers, and that made me feel so dirty and so good, even though I'd just finished. Then she sat down on the hall chair, pulled her knickers aside and told me to eat her out. I did it, down on my knees for her with the skirt still on and the spunk all over my cock, licking her cunt until she'd come. I don't know how many more times we had sex that night, but it was something like four or five, and all the time she made me keep the skirt on.

It was after that she took me on my first buying expedition. She was the boss by then, in bed, and for anything to do with bed, and although I was still fighting it and no way on earth was I going to tell my mates, I couldn't help but like it. When she told me we were going to go out and buy a skirt for me I knew straight away I had to do it. I will remember that day for the rest of my life.

I always found it slightly embarrassing shopping for lingerie for girlfriends, especially in some big smart department store, I suppose every bloke does, but imagine when the clothes are for you. It seemed like all the girls knew, and were laughing behind their hands to think of me in women's clothes, but Louise loved it. She was even holding stuff up against me to see if it would fit, and if she could have got away with it she would have taken me in the changing rooms and made me try stuff on.

All my life I've been a sucker for a pretty girl, the sort of guy who'll always pay for everything and happily do household chores and stuff to make a girlfriend happy. Not surprisingly perhaps I never did too well as a teenager, getting sent to do stuff or buy things for some pretty girl only to find out she'd gone with some bit of rough who treated her like dirt. With Louise it was worse. I couldn't resist, and just to have her attention was bliss, whatever it meant.

She thrived on it, and the more flustered and horny I got the more she loved it. We'd meant to buy a skirt, but I came out of that store with a full outfit, all chosen by her. It was all smart stuff, the sort of thing she wore to the office, hold-up stockings, black silk knickers and a matching bra, a white blouse in lightweight cotton so my bra would show through, a tight black knee-length skirt and a tailored jacket. We'd been to the make-up department too, and I'd stood there staring as she selected lipstick and eye-liner, nail polish and blusher, and a lot of other stuff I'd never even heard of. She even made me buy heels, the largest size they had, in black just like her own.

All the way home I was thinking of how it would feel to dress up, and there was no question that it was going to happen, right away. She always liked to tease though, and she never did things by halves. First she made me shower, watching all the time but never touching and fully dressed while I was naked. Then I had to shave myself, completely, my legs, my chest, my armpits, even my pubic hair.

I was hard long before I'd finished, and I had that odd helpless feeling again, like I always did when I gave up control to her completely. If she'd let me I'd have had her then and there, but she wasn't rushing. She made me dry myself off, never touching me, even when she made me bend over to have my bottom and balls talced. When I was done she gave me an inspection, then took me into the bedroom.

She told me what to do, exactly. First I had to take everything out of the wrappings and lay it out on the bed, very tidy. Just seeing what I was going to be wearing nearly made me come, and when she told me to put the knickers on, oh boy! She'd said I wasn't allowed to touch myself too, and I obeyed, sliding on those tiny silky knickers, up my legs and around my cock and balls, which wouldn't fit at all, but were bulging out on all sides.

Putting on the panties was the best bit, but only because I couldn't get any more horny. Louise continued giving orders, telling me exactly how to put each piece of clothing on. My bra felt strange, but no stranger than the thought of knowing it was *my* bra. Me, a man, owning a bra, and girl's knickers too. I was wearing bra and knickers, *my* bra and knickers. After that it was like I was becoming a new person.

Louise made me sit down at her dressing table in just my bra and knickers, and made me up, not as a travesty of a woman with bright red lipstick and over-the-top eye make-up, but the way she did herself, feminine but not tarty. I could barely recognise myself in the mirror, but I was a long way from complete. She sat back to watch again as I pulled on my stockings and blouse, then stood to get into my skirt, jacket, and at last my shoes. With that last detail she nodded, looking at me in approval and with her eyes full of want.

She had me, right there on the bed, there's no other description for it. OK, so my cock still went into her cunt, but she was completely in control. I got pushed back on the bed and she straddled me, tugging her skirt up with one hand and pulling her knickers aside to rub herself on the bulge in my own skirt. There was no resistance in me at all. I wanted it, but I felt like I was surrendering myself, maybe like a woman does when she wants sex and the man is on top of her and now it's going to happen whatever.

That's how I felt with Louise when she was pleasuring herself on me, and if she'd come like that I suppose I'd have gone and tossed myself off in the loo or something. She didn't. She pushed up my skirt and got my cock out of my knickers, pulling them down at the front so my balls were squashed up in a packet of silk. She climbed on and held my cock against herself, rubbing it all over her cunt before putting it up the hole. She fucked me, riding my cock and rubbing herself on my body until she came.

I could have come so easily, really at any moment since putting on my brand-new knickers. But I hadn't. I wanted to please her, to let her come first. I wanted to be the passive partner, maybe not the way women are today, because I wouldn't call any of my girlfriends exactly passive, but the old-fashioned way a woman was supposed to be, putting her man first. I'd have come with her if I could, but I didn't make it, and as she lifted off me I was left to take my cock in my hand and jerk off.

I could feel the silky knickers on my balls, and I wanted more of it, and to do it in front of her. So I pulled up the front of my knickers and wrapped them around my cock, feeling the silk against my skin and watching Louise's face as she looked down on me with a cruel little smile. I came so hard I thought I'd burst, and it went all over me, all over my hand and my knickers and my bra where Louise had pushed up my blouse as she rode me.

What she did then I will never forget. She was smiling, so cruel, and full of contempt for the state I was in, even laughing at me as she began to scrape up bits of spunk on her finger.

'Open wide,' she said, and I did.

'Eat it,' she said, and put the finger in my mouth.

I swear she looked like the devil as she watched me suck my own spunk off her finger, and that was just the way I wanted it, to be her plaything. She made me eat it all too, off her fingers and off my own. She even told me that she'd have made me suck my own cock clean if

37

I'd been able to, and do you know what? I enjoyed every second of it.

Nothing was the same after that. Everyone around us thought we were just a normal couple, maybe even a bit boring, because I never bragged about my sex life or how hot she was or anything like that. That was private. But as soon as we were alone in the flat she would tell me to get into my outfit and off we'd go. It wasn't just sex either, it was so much more.

On a typical evening we would both come in from work at more or less the same time. She might be there first, sitting in her favourite chair with her feet up and her shoes off, reading the paper. I'd come in and she'd give me a minute to relax before telling me to get changed, although I'd have been thinking about it all day and couldn't wait to do it. I'd go upstairs and lay my clothes out, sometimes the smart set we'd bought the first time, sometimes my blue skirt with the belt, sometimes my pink dress, and any one of a growing collection of matching bras and knickers.

Louise was teaching me to make-up, and I was slowly getting the hang of it, at least enough not to need to bother her every evening. I'd bought myself a wig too, shoulder-length and mid-brown, because we both agreed I should be a brunette. All of it, from the moment I began to undress and strip away my masculine exterior, to the moment I came downstairs as a woman, relaxed me in a way I could never explain to anyone who didn't feel the same. All my worries, all the stresses of work, just disappeared. I'd become somebody else, a woman who was cared for in the traditional feminine role, and as my side of the bargain I looked after Louise.

Fully transformed, I would come downstairs and fetch her a drink, usually a glass of white wine, then go about my chores. It seems stupid, maybe to most people, but I used to love that, hoovering, washing up, cooking, cleaning, all of it felt good, it felt like it was me. It turned me on too, just doing ordinary things as a woman, even if Louise wasn't in the mood, and it was always strictly understood that if she didn't want sex, it didn't happen.

That was rare, fortunately. Usually, by the time we'd finished eating and I'd done the washing up she'd be ready. She always liked a glass of wine, and she'd be sitting in her chair, looking like a million pounds in her smart work clothes, sipping her wine. Sometimes she'd make me lie on the floor and play with myself in front of her until she was ready, then she'd mount me and fuck me. Sometimes she'd just tell me to get down on my knees and crawl to her, then adjust herself in the chair, with one long leg thrown over the arm and her knickers pulled aside so I could lick her.

Whatever happened, she always came first, and I was always made to do it in my hand and eat what came out. She loved that. She loved to watch and to tell me how she'd never done that and never would, not for any man. She used to laugh at me too, while I was wanking and while I was eating it afterwards, and I loved every second of it. I even loved the spankings, 'cause while it stung like anything it made me feel I was hers.

We lived like that for nearly a year, and I never grew tired of it, especially as there were always new outfits to buy and new things to do. At one point she decided I ought to know how it felt to be a tart. She took me to a sex shop and actually told the female assistant that I was into cross-dressing and what I needed. They had a great time, the two of them, choosing scarlet underwear, a peep-hole bra and a pair of split-crotch panties so that my cock and balls hung out at the front. On top of that went a little pink frou-frou skirt and a crop-top to match. There were suspenders with the undies too, and I got those and some scarlet fishnets, and four-inch heels in lipstick red.

They made me dress up in it, right there in the shop, and when I was ready Louise ordered me to come out of the changing room and show off, in front of other customers, men and women too. I'd started getting erect by then, 'cause I just couldn't help it, but because she was an angel she took me back in the changing room and tossed me off into a tissue.

It could have lasted, I know it could, but there was one problem. I knew I could never be a real woman, but I wanted to be as close as possible in every way. Most of all I wanted a name for Louise to use when we were alone, something plain like Mary or Jane. She didn't want that. What she wanted was for me to be a man dressed as a woman, because what she really got a kick out of was humiliating me.

So I did a really, really stupid thing. I went to a pro to try and get what I needed. She was crap anyway, just going through the motions really, but inevitably Louise found out, and that was that. She felt I'd betrayed her, and that was that. I'd broken her trust and she didn't feel she could be with me any more. Now she's with a guy from her work, and I still see them occasionally at the tube station. They look normal, like any other couple, but I always wonder if the moment they're home he's going to be slipping on a pair of silky knickers and a lacy bra.

– *Edward, Basingstoke, UK*

Second Flute

You think I'm so prim. Every night this week I've seen you in the front row looking up at me with those hopeful eyes. Your mouth has fallen open and you look like an imbecile, but you don't even realise.

The orchestra is on top form tonight but Beethoven's genius is lost on you, isn't it, pervert? Your mind is somewhere else entirely. There's a movie playing in your head right now, and I'm the star. What am I doing this time? Am I naked? No? Still in my heels and nylons? Yes, that's it, heels and nylons and a big thick cock in my mouth! Gosh, it excites you so much to picture me acting like a slut. Such a conservative-looking girl, that's how I seem to you, in my black satin concert dress and subtle make-up.

You probably think I go home at night to some limp wrist of a husband and spend the evening looking at fabric samples for the new conservatory. If I were to step off the stage right now and whisper the truth in your ear, I swear you'd stiffen up like a church candle.

You'd be horrified if you knew how I got this job. Horrified, but just a little bit thrilled. I almost wish you did know. I'd like to see the look on your face. Watch your strawberry soft-centre harden into animal lust.

Securing a regular position with an orchestra isn't easy you know, especially for a flute player like me. The supply of slightly posh, winsome girls far outstrips the demand. It's not enough just to be technically proficient. No, to break free of the competition a girl needs to know who to impress and how.

Each orchestra has its director, the Maestro. He's not much use to me on stage (I find all the waving rather distracting and prefer to keep my nose in the sheet music), but in one respect he's the focus of all my attention. You see, the Maestro is my ticket to regular employment and I'll do whatever it takes to manipulate him into giving me what I want.

I learned the ropes early on, during my very first professional engagement. I had graduated from the Royal Academy six months previously and was getting sick to death of low-paid session work when a second flute position suddenly became available with a major London orchestra. I telephoned to arrange an audition, and a week later I was pacing up and down in the rehearsal room waiting to be called.

You ought to know that being nervous makes me horny. I've often wondered why. Whenever something important is about to happen, something serious that requires all my attention, my mind starts to gravitate hopelessly towards sex. And then I think to myself 'you slut, how can you think about sex at a time like this?' and that thought makes me feel even sexier and sluttier, and so it goes on until finally I have to run off and find a private place to take care of myself. I think that's my favourite way to do it, really quick and under pressure. Fully-clothed and standing with my bottom pressed up against a wall, I'll hitch up my skirt with one hand whilst the painted fingers of the other rub my clit into submission.

But I'm getting sidetracked. Back to the rehearsal room. As the adrenaline started to pump through my system, boosting my heart rate and heightening my senses, I approached a state of almost painful arousal. I had to fight the urge to teeter into the bathroom and give my pussy a little attention. Glancing around the room, I could find no evidence that any of the other girls were similarly afflicted. Rather, they seemed entirely calm and focused on the task in hand. A few I recognised from college, snooty types in ballerina pumps and Monsoon knitwear. My sloppy technique, I knew, was no match for theirs. But it occurred to me that maybe I could fight them on more favourable turf?

You see, despite their impeccable grooming, they were all virtually sexless. Not a pheromone between them. I may not have been the best flute player in that room, but I was most certainly the horniest. And I started to think that maybe I could turn my damp knickers to my advantage. I'm terribly sly like that.

The orchestra's Russian Maestro had a bit of a reputation for dealing harshly with the younger ladies in the orchestra. I knew the type: mid-fifties, imposing physique, young mousy-looking wife. He had that cruel glint in his eye that distinguishes all 1970s graduates of the Moscow Conservatoire, and his infamous temper tantrums could reduce an entire string section to snivelling blancmange in an instant. My lacklustre rendition of Chaminade's *Concertino* was unlikely to prompt anything other than a dry put-down, but I was determined to give him at least one good reason to take me seriously.

Either fate or intuition had prompted me to dress the part that morning. I'd chosen a short A-line skirt to expose long legs sheathed in sheer natural tights and knee-boots, with a tight T-shirt to show off my tiny waist and small tender tits. My long dark hair was tidily trussed up in its usual French plait and I had given my eyes a few layers of mascara to perfect my favoured look of doe-eyed innocence.

As I opened the door to the concert hall I saw the Maestro leaning against the piano, his face already a mask of frustration (I had procrastinated for a while after my name was called to ensure that I was a little late). I contrived to look flustered and tottered over to where he stood, apologising as I went. When I was close enough to reach out and touch him I bowed my head slightly and gazed up with an expression that suggested contrition, but with more than a hint of wilfulness.

'My name's Dora,' I said. 'So sorry I'm late. I do hope you won't think badly of me, it's just that I get so nervous when I do auditions. I've been trying awfully hard to calm down but I really couldn't do it on my own so one of the other girls gave me a nip of whisky to take the edge off. I'm afraid I might be a tiny bit tipsy.' I punctuated that last sentence with a self-induced hiccup, and followed it with a giggle for effect.

The Maestro clapped his hand to his mouth and slumped onto the piano stool in shock. I don't suppose he'd ever been treated with such disrespect before.

'You English girls never cease to amaze me.' He spat the words in a thick Russian accent. 'For twenty years I perfect my craft, I cut my teeth on the world's greatest orchestras, and finally I come to London to discover what treasures this country has to offer and what is happening? I am faced with a drunk little tart!' I noticed a vein begin to throb at his temple. 'Who arrives *late*, and then talks to me as if I am the music director of some cheap wedding band!'

Taking a chance, I decided to ratchet up the tension a stage further. 'Oh dear,' I said with an over-familiar wink, 'someone got out of bed on the wrong side this morning.'

The Maestro's face contorted with rage as he unsuccessfully searched his vocabulary for a powerful enough expletive. Losing his battle for control, he raised his right hand high above his head and swept it down hard in an arc, connecting resoundingly with the wooden panel of the piano stool beneath him.

Blam! The hollow sound reverberated around us for an age, eventually giving way to a tense silence.

We held each other's gaze for a moment, and then I deliberately dropped my eyes to his lap where I noticed an unmistakeable stirring. Without attempting to disguise my scrutiny of the growing protrusion in his exquisitely-tailored trousers, I whispered, 'You're right Maestro, my behaviour just now was unacceptable. I've been warned many times before but somehow I never seem to learn my lesson.'

As I finished speaking I looked up once again. His face was no less animated than before but there had been a subtle shift away from anger, to desire. With his eyes he posed the question, 'Are you seriously up for this?'

I hesitated for a fraction of a second, but my ambition trampled any reservations I might have had. I stepped carefully to his right, bent forwards over the keyboard and rested my hands and face on the piano's dark varnished lid.

He began to visibly perspire. Under his breath, he whispered, 'Just look at you, poking your bottom out in my face you dirty, cheap little girl.' The put-downs didn't bother me, I was focused on that second flute chair. And in any case, the sight of his growing erection was making the lips of my pussy slick with a sweet honey that I could feel as it soaked through the gauze of my knickers and into the sheer fabric of my tights.

The Maestro rose to stand behind me and take in the view. 'You know that your skirt is sticking right up don't you? Oh and it's making you wet isn't it, knowing that I'm looking at your bottom crammed tight into those ridiculous tart's panties.' I heard him undo his zip to free his cock, and assumed from his rhythmic sighs that he'd begun quietly beating its length through his hand. The mental image drove me wild.

'I bet you want me to go further don't you, you want me to really shame you, look right at your bare cunt and rub myself all over your little white ass, that's what you want isn't it?'

I wriggled from foot to foot in encouragement. This was turning out exactly how I'd hoped it would. I was exploiting his weakness to the full, and getting hornier by the minute.

I heard him take a step forward and felt rough hands reach up under my skirt, yank my tights and knickers down to my knees and then pull my skirt high up over my waist. There was a brief rustle and then the silky feel of fabric binding itself around my wrists, holding them fast to the piano strings below. I looked up. He'd used his tie.

That was when I finally started to feel vulnerable, all tied up and exposed. There was no getting out of this now, no going back. Unable to run or move my arms, and with my naked sex splayed out and ready to be taken, I felt my heart pounding in my chest and my desire for penetration became almost unbearable. Was I actually going to fuck him? I hadn't quite thought that far ahead, but soon I wouldn't have any choice in the matter.

'I'm looking right up your little pink cunt,' he whispered. 'I've got my big hard cock in my hands and I'm looking at your cunt and I know you want me to pound it right into you. You want me to stretch it really wide and fill you up with cream.'

His filthy tongue drove out the last remnants of decency from my mind. 'I do, I want it.'

'Louder!' he ordered. 'Don't start playing the innocent girly now, admit that you're a slut and you need my cock!'

'Yes! I'm a slut and I need cock, I need it in my pussy!' I cried, and felt the blunt head of something impossibly thick and muscular press itself into the opening of my sex. The exquisite pain of violation and the thought of all the pre-cum glistening on the tip of his phallus almost brought me off at that point. But, to my dismay, he mastered himself and withdrew. I moaned in frustration.

'Oh no,' he began, leaning in to whisper right in my ear. 'I'm not going to lose my head like that over your easy pussy. I'll make you feel my strength up there, but not like that, not the way that you want it. I can see that you're enjoying this far too much and I'm supposed to be showing you the error of your ways.' He had me there.

I felt the fingers of one hand hook themselves into my plait and pull my face up into the light. He wanted to show me something. With his other hand he reached into the recesses of the piano and drew out a metre-long wooden ruler, the old-fashioned kind they used to have in schools. His forward-planning was impressive, but why was I surprised? I don't suppose you get to reach his elevated status in life without being prepared.

'You like?' he asked.

I nodded nervously.

'You shouldn't, Babushka here has a proud history of disciplining slutty second flutes like you.'

I had to admit, the idea of really being punished for my sins against meritocracy gave me a peculiar thrill, but Babushka looked like a serious piece of equipment.

I wondered if I hadn't bitten off a little more than I could chew. But there was no time for second thoughts, because in an instant he withdrew the ruler from my view and pressed my face back down against the piano. Tingling with apprehension, and still wishing he'd stop messing about and just put that hard cock up inside me, I heard the ruler swish through the air and land lightly against the top of my thighs. A practice stroke? The next one answered my question.

Crack! A lightning bolt of white-hot agony struck across my thighs, flashing down each leg to the ends of my hot, painted toes. Before I could even gasp, another hit. Crack! This time higher, stinging against my sex, and then *crack!* Right across the fullest part of my bottom. I managed not to cry out, but couldn't suppress the tears that scorched down my cheeks, due more to shock than anything else.

I heard the Maestro pacing behind me, I could feel his eyes on my tortured cheeks, scrutinising them closely.

'That's brought you up nicely now. I wish you could see the pretty pink and purple flecks all over your bottom, it's really very attractive. I must admit, I get a little excited by the sight of a hot wet pussy poking out between bruised tender thighs.'

'You bastard, you bastard,' I groaned, still reeling from the painful onslaught. I suddenly felt pitiful, and humiliated. A silly little girl who got mixed up in adult games and couldn't take the heat.

'Well done, second flute. You've taken your punishment admirably well. All you must do is thank me now, and I'll take off that little pussy of yours.'

Momentarily dumbfounded, I gave a snort to indicate my unwillingness to comply, but as I did so, a warm rush of endorphins rushed to my behind and intensified my lust once more. My pride disintegrated.

'Thank you, Maestro, thank you, please just fuck me,' I begged, and in response his breathing became rhythmic and I heard him once again pummelling his thick shaft through his hands, this time right up against me. Finally, I heard him moan and felt the full length of his cock spear right up to my womb, quick hard thrusts at first, and then a steady pounding that rocked my whole pelvis back and forth against the piano keyboard.

I felt so stretched and full, so wretched, so dirty and sluttish. I couldn't hold back and screamed for him to let go, and he did, firing shot after shot of scalding cream deep inside. My legs gave way beneath me as I came, but the Maestro took the weight of my hips in his hands and held me tight as the climax shuddered through me.

When I eventually regained my balance, he untied me and we tidied ourselves up in silence. As he left, he called over his shoulder. 'The position is yours, of course. I assume you can actually play?' I nodded. 'Don't let me down again,' he said, and closed the door behind him.

I looked over at my flute, which remained innocently in its case. It looked back at me with its solitary eye . . . accusingly, I thought.

That was the first time, and there were plenty more to follow. Take the American orchestra I joined briefly a few summers back. Now he was a weird one! By then I had a pretty long rap sheet, as they say over there, and it had become clear that my reputation preceded me. I was getting used to the Maestro just asking for it up front when I walked through the door. 'Hello, my dear, coming to audition for second flute? Lovely, get comfortable down here on your knees and I'll feed you my cock when you're ready.' I exaggerate, but not much.

That's how I assumed things would go with the American Maestro, especially when I heard that the audition was to take place at his house. I'd done my best to find out what his peccadillos were, but it had proved difficult. All I knew was that he was unmarried, definitely wasn't into boys, and fancied himself as 'camp counsellor'. You know, 'I'm here to unlock *your* potential, to let *you* show *me* how *you're* special.' I didn't buy the vanilla front, I never do these days.

I picked an outfit that I thought would be a safe enough bet. Glossy black skyscraper heels, ultra-sheer black seamed nylons, super-tight pencil skirt and a paper-thin white blouse. I doused myself from head to toe in expensive scent and painted my lips, fingers and toes all in the same dangerous colour of red. Just getting dressed up all tarty got me a little breathless. The adrenaline was going to work on my pussy in its usual way, and there's something just so naughty about dressing up to please a stranger's cock. That's probably why I removed my bra and knickers before I left.

When I arrived, the Maestro opened the door and welcomed me into his home with a broad smile and a vigorous handshake. He was one of those big brisk men with floppy blond hair that they must make on a production line somewhere on the east coast. Thick-set, but in a muscular sort of way, he towered over my 5ft 4 and had a pinkish glow in his cheeks that I guessed came from healthy outdoor pursuits rather than neat spirits.

'Excellent, excellent!' he exclaimed. 'You must be Dora, so lovely to meet you.'

He led me into his lounge, sat down, and motioned for me to stand in the far corner of the room.

'I've set the music stand up over by the window,' he explained. 'When you're ready, I'd like to hear your first piece.'

I must have looked stunned. This was the first time I'd actually been asked to play my flute at an audition for almost a decade.

Hesitantly, I assembled my flute, smoothed my sheet music out on the stand and blew through the first few bars. I was getting anxious now, maybe this one wasn't in the bag? Eventually he called out for me to stop, and then fell silent for a few moments, with his eyes on the carpet and fingers pressed to his mouth as if in deep thought.

'Dora,' he said eventually, looking up to show me his best caring-yet-serious face, 'I think you have the potential to play a lot better than this.'

'Oh?' I raised an eyebrow.

'I really think you could.' He opened his hands wide, as if to indicate the size of the fish he'd thrown back. 'I'm looking at Dora right now and I can see from her sexy clothes and her proud stance that she's a feisty confident woman, but I'm afraid she's not communicating any of that to me with her playing.'

He shook his head and stuck out his lower lip, just to clarify that Dora not reaching her potential was a *bad* thing. I wanted desperately to laugh, but managed to disguise it with a cough.

'I'm sure I'm doing the best I can,' I said, my face framed in mock concern. 'Do you have any suggestions as to how I might improve my performance?'

'Well now . . . you know, I think I might? You see, some years ago I had a very similar young girl come to audition for me and we had rather a lot of success with certain exercises.' He flushed and licked his lips. 'Nothing too "out there"' – as he made the quotation marks with his fingers in the air, I shuddered – 'just confidence-building stuff, the kinda thing they have actors and opera singers do, you know what I mean?'

Dear God, I thought, I'm going to spend all night shouting out positive affirmations for this tosser when all I wanted was a nice hard cock and some guaranteed work for a few months.

'OK,' I said, resigning myself to my fate. 'I'm all yours, Maestro, do your worst.'

'What a great attitude! I'll explain my reasoning to you, and then perhaps we can try out a few little scenarios.' It was a statement more than a suggestion.

He licked his lips and fixed the full beam of his blue eyes on my own. 'It is my belief that most people fail to reach their potential as performers because of some latent inhibition. You Brits are especially afflicted. Up there on stage you want to give it your all but embarrassment makes you hold something back. You're scared to show that dark emotional side to yourself. But we need to see it, we need to feel *you*. Right now, *I* need to feel *Dora*.' He looked at me expectantly.

Somewhere deep inside me, a light came on. I formed my features into an expression of docile trust: 'Gosh, that's interesting. So how do you think I should go about freeing myself from my inhibitions?'

'Ah ha, yes,' he said, 'in your case, I think we'll need to do something quite radical.'

He looked away and began to fidget. 'Is there any other situation, say a personal one, where your inhibitions get in the way?'

I pretended to think hard, and said, 'Well, I don't want to shock you, Maestro, but I suppose my sex life would be a good example.'

He whipped his head back round to face me and beamed. 'Good, good! Well that's as good a place as any to start. Why don't you tell me a little about your inhibitions in that situation?'

Feigning hesitancy, I made my voice quaver a little as I said, 'Well, Maestro, I'm scared to do it with the light on, I get all embarrassed about my boyfriends looking at my body all naked, and my face all screwed up and ugly when I'm coming.'

'Really?' he stammered. 'And, do you find yourself unable to . . . ah . . . vocalise in those situations?'

'Oh yes, I just can't bear to open my mouth and say the nasty words they want me to.'

'Dear, dear, now isn't this an interesting parallel. I think that if we tackle one problem, we might just solve the other.'

I allowed my mouth to fall open in wonder.

'Let's take the vocalisation first. Just for the purposes of this little exercise, I'll pretend to be your boyfriend.' No surprises there.

'OK, Maestro, what's the situation?'

'Well, let's say we're in bed, we've had a lovely dinner and we're all cuddled up, now ask me what you want me to do to you.'

I drew myself up to my full height, planted my feet slightly apart and with my hands on my hips I said, 'Fuck me.'

'Right, yes, very good,' he said, apparently in some discomfort as he shifted in his seat.

'Fuck my pussy,' I continued slowly, rolling the words lovingly around my mouth. 'Fuck me till I'm screaming on the end of your big hard cock, you bastard.'

Remembering he was supposed to be in character, he stuttered, 'That's good to know, ahm . . . darling, but I just want you to be happy and feel comfortable.'

'Screw comfortable,' I continued, getting into my stride. 'I just want you to ruin me, pull my head on and off your cock and make me lick up every last drop of your cream.'

'Darling, err . . .' he made to interrupt, but the muse was with me.

'And then when you're all spent, I want you to sit nice and quiet downstairs while I get my pussy ridden over and over again by young hard cocks. Strangers I have to bring home when you can't give me enough. You'll sit there in the dark and listen to me telling them how much I love to suck on their meat and then screaming when they start to stretch me open.'

I relaxed my stance, softened my face and asked, 'Am I doing OK?'

The Maestro appeared somewhat taken aback, and he'd given up trying to disguise his erection.

'Bravo!' he said, 'and well done you for . . . really getting on board with this exercise, but I'm sorry, Dora, I find myself a little shamed here. I'm afraid I've been unable to control myself physically.' He finished with a nervous chuckle.

'Oh don't worry,' I said sweetly, 'it's only natural under the circumstances. Why don't you just slip it out and make yourself a little more comfortable, I really wouldn't mind.' Seeing his obvious relief, I decided to take matters into my own hands. I crossed the room, dropped elegantly to my knees and unbuttoned his expensive jeans to free up his impressively-proportioned cock.

'Goodness,' I said, 'don't my nails look pretty against your skin like that?'

He failed to answer but I felt him grow yet more rigid under my fingers before I withdrew my hand and climbed back onto my feet.

He looked from my face, to his cock, and then back to my face. He appeared to struggle with some inner demon, and then blurted out, 'It looks to me like we've made enough progress with your vocal issues, I think it's about time we moved on to the physical problems and your desire to hide your body.'

'OK' I said, my face a picture of innocence. 'Do you think some more role-play will help?'

'Yes I think it would, but this time I need you to stop relying on your mouth to lead the way. Try showing me with your body. Show me' – he corrected himself – 'I mean to say, show your boyfriend, what you like, what you want him to do.'

'I'll do my best.'

I began to slowly unbutton my blouse, fixing my eyes on his cock to gauge his interest. Only a semi at the moment as he wasn't sure how far I would take it.

As I eased the slight fabric over my shoulders to expose my soft white breasts it maintained its position, twitching gently when I licked my finger and rubbed it over the tip of each dark nipple, blowing on them to get them harder and pointier. He liked this, but we weren't in the right area yet. I decided to try a different tack.

Walking into the centre of the room, I positioned a chair in front of the Maestro, planted my bottom on the edge of the seat and crossed my right leg over my left. Leaning down, I gently eased the hard patent leather of my shoe away from my foot to expose five perfect little toes in their cradle of shimmering nylon. I looked up and saw that his cock was firming up. Maybe this was the money shot?

Thanking God for the dexterity he'd blessed me with, I smoothed my hands slowly down my leg, around my ankle and under the sole of my foot, lifting it eagerly to my mouth. I snaked out my tongue and with eyes closed in bliss began to lap lovingly at my toes, finally taking my biggest toe into my mouth and sucking on it hungrily.

The sight of his straining cock and the sensation of my tongue against my slippery feet began to get me all breathless and aroused again. As I continued with my leg show I became aware of a fresh slick of moisture between my legs, accompanied by an urgent need for contact. He was getting off on this, I could tell, but I wanted to take things further and I was sure that I could get that cock even harder somehow.

I pointed at his cock and mimed a handjob. He got the idea, and started to rub himself, hesitantly at first, but then harder and harder, his face contorted as he began to lose control.

Instinctively I knew what he wanted to see, and what I wanted to take. I stood up, slipped out of my skirt, and posed in front of him, naked but for my nylons, wispy garter belt and one remaining spike-heel. Stepping close enough to touch his legs with my own, I parted my legs and showed him the wetness glistening on my downy sex. I saw him clench the muscles at the base of his cock to hold back the inevitable. I was glad of his restraint, I wanted that hot cream for myself.

I turned around, dropped onto all fours and let him take in the sight of my splayed sex, quivering bottom and the dark pink bud of my anus. I heard him moan and whisper, 'Lord no, what are you doing to me, I can't stop myself.'

It wouldn't take much now, just one more hint. Reaching behind me with one hand, I pushed two fingers deep into my sex, the overwhelming sensation making me weak for a moment as I felt the walls of my pussy spasm powerfully around me. With difficulty, I pulled my fingers out and stroked them upwards to my hard little ring. Moistening it, I prepared myself for the onslaught.

That was it. When I heard him cry out, 'Oh you dirty bitch, that's it, you're going to get it like a whore,' I knew I had successfully trampled over the caring façade.

I felt triumphant. Elated. Hot blood rushed to my hole as he broke it open with his cock. Pushing my face into the floor, he took my ass mercilessly, his full length beating into me and sending pulses of electricity from deep up inside my rectum to the tip of my clit.

After a few deep thrusts I could hold back no longer and let myself shake into climax. He was hot on my heels, and I felt his phallus pump itself into my tummy as I lay, dizzy and shivering beneath him.

He never looked me in the eye again. But I still got the position. I always get what I want. Next year I think I want to be first flute. I'll just have to raise my game.

– Dora, London, UK

In the Crowd

I like to go to live gigs, usually with my friend Amy. We do goth, metal, emo, that sort of thing, but other stuff too. I got tickets for the Led Zep reunion tour, believe it or not. Then there was this time we went to see . . .

Maybe I shouldn't say.

You've probably heard of them in a vague way. If you're into industrial or heavy music at all you'll know they can sell out a stadium just like that. The lead singer is this huge beefy bloke with scary eyes under thick eyeliner. They sing in German, and it's powerful anthemic stuff that totally seizes you like no other music I've ever heard. Lots of shouted responses from the crowd, lots of pyrotechnics on stage. Flames and sweat and testosterone and the overpowering feeling you're in danger of surrendering your soul to them.

So we were there in the mosh-pit – the stalls you'd call it if they hadn't taken the seats out – not too close to the front because despite having our biggest boots on we were still shorter than the men in the crowd and likely to get crushed if we got too far forward. We'd had to run to claim this spot. Anyway, as the support band left the stage Amy decided she needed the toilet. Desperately. She'd made the mistake of having a pint before we queued to get in.

'Your timing stinks!' I complained. 'I'm not missing this!'

If she'd been a bloke she would have used an empty plastic bottle, but she was too shy so she scrambled off through the crowd, promising to meet me later. And I was left on my own.

I wasn't worried, just a bit annoyed. I had a good line of sight between two sets of shoulders to the stage. I had my New Rock boots on, so I wasn't bothered about getting my toes stamped on – the first rule of concert-going: wear big steel-toed boots. (The second rule is Don't Drink Pints.) The New Rocks, all black leather and steel plates and buckles, looked like something from a Manga comic and gave me a good couple of extra inches' height. And above them I was wearing artfully-torn fishnet stockings and a short leather skirt and a tight sleeveless top over a push-up bra that gave me a jutting cleavage. All in black, of course, just like almost everyone else in the crowd. I looked good, I know that, but no one was there to look at me. We were fixated on the stage.

The band came on before Amy reappeared, and at that point I forgot about her. It was an amazing show. Plumes of fire and dry ice billowed over our heads; you could feel the heat. The microphones burst into flames. Guitar riffs sounded like machine-gun fire. And that music! – majestic, arrogant, almost horrifying. The crowd went mental, heaving and shouting and waving our arms like a single being. I sang along with every song and swayed along with the crowd, transported by the music. As the set went on we lost ourselves altogether.

There was no chance of keeping a discreet distance from people in that press, of course. We were all bumping arms and shoulders, all hot and sticky with excitement. It took a while for me to notice that there was someone getting just that little bit too close. He was directly behind me, and though I didn't look I knew it was a man because he was brushing up against my bum repeatedly, and he was hard. I mean it, he had a stiff one. I could feel it jabbing at the soft curve of my bottom. His chest brushed my back too. He had broader shoulders than me; that was all I could tell without turning round.

Dirty bastard.

Don't think I'd put up with that sort of thing normally. This was a total stranger taking advantage of the crowd for a bit of filthy fun, and I'm no slag. I don't like guys who get too pushy and take stuff for granted. But somehow this was different. I was high on the pounding music. I was delirious with adrenaline. I wasn't me for the moment, not properly. So I didn't pull away. I understood why he was hard; if I'd been a bloke I'd have been standing proud too, throbbing with the beat. As it was my knickers were damp, my pussy all swollen. I stood my ground and let him press up against me and then withdraw. There was a rush of heat to my sex. It just seemed part of the heady experience we were all caught up in.

I didn't turn round.

After the first couple of brushes, he knew I was aware of him, knew I was letting him get away with it. He got bolder. He put his hands on the back of my hips, lightly, and brushed up against the whole line of my body. I kept my eyes on the stage. As the crowd swayed he pressed closer into me. I could feel the hard ridge of his concealed cock sliding across the leather of my skirt. I felt him put one hand on my bum cheek and squeeze, enjoying the firm flesh. Testing me, I guess. Then he began to rub my butt with his open palm.

60

I wriggled against him.

God, this was weird. Half my attention was on the stage, half on what was happening to my body. Despite the muggy heat my nipples were tightening to points, sticking out through my cotton top. I felt dizzy, not sure how this could be happening to me, how I could be permitting it.

The lead singer was crouched, hammering on his thigh as he roared into the microphone.

The guy behind me dipped his hand to the edge of my skirt, and when he swept it up again he came up under the leather, skin on skin, his palm on my bare cheek. He had dry hard hands. He found the edge of my knickers and slid his fingers under the trim. I felt his nails on my skin.

I looked to either side then, trying to be casual. None of my neighbours seemed to be taking any notice of what was going on in the shadows below head-level. Down there a finger slid up and down the cleft of my bum. His other hand had vanished from my hip; all I had was that tickling tease of a finger. It almost hypnotised me – until he pulled my skirt right up and pressed something hot to the cool flesh of my bottom. I nearly fell into the people in front of me, only he grabbed me by the waist in time. He had his cock out in public, for Chrissake! And was rubbing it against me under my skirt!

That thick hot cylinder nearly freaked me out. To be touched by a totally anonymous cock, one I hadn't even seen . . .

To be used for my arse, by this nameless meat.

I could feel the teeth of his fly zip. I could feel wisps of his hair. I looked down and saw his fingers where he held me. Ringless, anonymous hands too, with blunt clean nails. He was wearing a long-sleeved black T-shirt too, so I couldn't see what his arms were like. He held me firmly against him, and his cock twitched impatiently as I caught my breath again.

Back and forth he rolled his cock across my bottom, from cheek to cheek, rubbing it against me. Rubbing it into the dip between the swells of flesh. It felt smooth and warm and hard enough to send a tingle right through me, imagining what he could do with that hard tool. Then, pushing it firmly down, he slid it along the gusset of my knickers. They were soaking wet by now – and not just from the heat either – there between my closed thighs. He had to flex his legs to get down there, pushing hard into the slot between thighs and pussy lips. I wasn't making it easy for him. I was keeping it tight.

I could feel the warmth of his breath on the back of my neck.

There was too much friction against the lace, I guess. So he used his fingertips to pull my knickers down, baring my bottom properly. Just as far as my thighs, though. I could feel the straining elastic biting into me. I could feel how damp the cloth was on the inside of my leg. I could feel how juicy my pussy was, now that it was bare, and heat rushed up my whole body.

Bare-arsed in a crowd of thousands . . .

He ran his fingers down my secret slash, stroking my sensitive bum-hole, my fuzz of hair, my swollen pussy-lips. He found how slippery I was, how sticky and eager for his touch. He made me squirm for him. Then where his fingers had gone, his cock followed.

He couldn't shove it inside me, not without bending me right forward; the angle was all wrong. So he just stroked back and forth along my slot, between my thighs, in the wet and the heat.

'*Ich will*,' thundered the lead singer on stage: I want.

I knew what the man behind me wanted. And I knew what I wanted. I wanted to be fucked right here, though it wasn't this man I wanted, whoever he was. His identity didn't matter. I didn't look round because I didn't want to see what he looked like; whatever it was it would be a disappointment. I wanted that thick anonymous cock. I wanted to be taken advantage of. I wanted to be fucked by the lead singer up there. I wanted to be fucked by the music.

His movement became faster, more frantic.

I crumpled up the front of my skirt to touch myself, fingering my clit. He put one hand over mine, to feel what I was doing. He put his other arm around me, holding me close as he thrust. Our movements were swallowed in the swaying of the crowd. My panting wasn't audible. It was like being fucked by the whole lot of them, thousands strong. Fucked by the crowd.

I started to come, and the music was so loud that no one heard me crying out. My squeal was just part of the crowd's noise. My open mouth and flushed face were both just one more in the mob. But I heard his bellow because his lips were near my ear. His hand clenched over mine and then he splashed onto the inside of my leg, his thighs shaking with strain.

He held me tight for a moment afterwards. Then he let go.

I still didn't turn to look.

There were two more songs, then the encore which ran to four more. We got pushed round as a scuffle broke out to our left and we all backed off, the crowd swirling. Somewhere in the middle of that I hitched my knickers back up under my skirt. I could feel his jiz sliding down to my stocking-tops, sticky where my thighs moved together. My pulse beat in my swollen clit.

When the lights went up and it was all over I turned casually and glanced at the men behind me. Everyone was sweaty and bright-eyed and elated, grinning like maniacs despite their exhaustion. But no one tried to catch my eye. No one leered or laughed or winked at me.

He was gone.

I hadn't seen his face. Maybe he hadn't seen mine. And no one else had noticed, I guess. A good job too, I told myself. If they had, they might have figured that if one man could take his chance on me, why not more of them?

Now there's a thought. Maybe next time.

– Suzie, Hastings, UK

Taking the Gift

There was no particular reason why Camilla would have wanted to set me up, so it must have been Andy with Camilla's connivance. Andy Masters was my tutor at Cambridge, a tall don with a scarred cheek from rugby and long hair always in need of a wash and trim. He had insisted at our first meeting that I drop the Mr Masters and just call him Andy. He then gave me a book by Georges Bataille and at our weekly tutorials from then on we spent long afternoons discussing mysticism and sensuality; religious sacrifice; prostitution taboos and the usual jumble of philosophical fetishes and fixations.

Didn't Sartre say hell is other people?

That's what I was thinking as I waited alone in Dick's, the champagne bar in Knightsbridge. Camilla had told me to wear something *très* sexy and I was feeling self-conscious sitting there at the bar perched on a high stool in a low-cut red dress that was way too short in heels that were way too high. Camilla had suggested we meet to celebrate. She was graduating and, to my relief, I had survived my first year. We had gone to the same school, a convent set behind ivy-clad walls in the Kent countryside in what seemed like the 1930s, and when I arrived at Trinity Camilla took me under her wing.

It was mainly men in the bar – that's why it was called Dick's, I suppose, but there was a sprinkling of women dressed like me, close to naked with too much make-up and long bare legs tanned in the heat wave – it had touched 100 degrees Fahrenheit on the first day of July, a record by all accounts.

I paid £12 for a flute of champagne and examined my reflection in the mirror behind the bar. My lips were that shade of red that said danger, my green eyes looked glassy like old bottles, and my dark hair in the ivory lights had a gloss that made me feel, I don't know, *très* sexy. Even my expression was different, I thought, relief perhaps at being back in the real world beyond the quads and punts and cloisters of Cambridge.

The bubbles went up my nose with the first sip of champagne and I instantly felt giggly. I sent Camilla a text, drank my drink faster than was sensible, and sat there telling myself not to spend £12 on another glass.

I turned to look at the pianist, who had polished ebony skin like the black keys on his piano, and I realised that the man in the corner was staring at me, studying me, like you study your image in a shop when you're thinking of buying a new dress. He smiled. I flushed like a schoolgirl and he made a flapping motion, pointing at the stool next to me, pointing at himself, and I found myself nodding.

He was wearing a black suit like an undertaker and a silvery tie that glittered like a fish as he left his table. He lowered his head in an old-fashioned way as he sat on the stool beside me. He had dark eyes, a big moustache, coffee-coloured skin and long hands that he placed together on the bar.

It was at that very second that my phone rang. CAMILLA came up on the screen.

'Where are you?' I demanded.

'Darling, something terrible's happened.'

'What –'

'I can't tell you now. I'll tell you tomorrow, I'm rushing. Just, you know, go with the flow –'

'What?'

The phone was dead. I was sitting in a little red dress, legs twisting below me like snakes trying to get comfortable, and for some reason an essay by Georges Bataille on *The Object of Desire* slipped into my head like a warning or an invitation, I wasn't sure which, and I wasn't sure if that one glass of champagne had gone to my head and I was imagining things.

The man had sat there patiently through the phone call and now offered to buy another drink.

'Thank you.'

'Nahume,' he said, introducing himself. He was the same age as Andy Masters, dark and mysterious. It made me feel mysterious. Like my new name.

'Camilla,' I said.

'Agh, like the Queen.'

He smiled. He was looking into my eyes and turning his watch around his wrist. His wrist was hairy and the watch was gold with a heavy bracelet. I sipped the champagne. He continued turning the watch as he cast his eyes over my legs, my breasts, my collarbones, my lips. I held my back straight. I remember reading that the secret of grace is to be poised not posed.

'We go?' he said.

It was all so quick. So easy. I was playing a role. A game. Running through my head was a tickertape like you see on the bottom of the television news, a long explanation that I wasn't what he thought I was, and at the same time I recalled a quote from Bataille, a line I had scored in yellow with a marker pen and would look up later: *Not every woman is a potential prostitute, but*

67

prostitution is the logical consequence of the female attitude.

A glass of champers is all it takes, I thought as I slipped from the stool. Nahume placed two £20 notes in the silver saucer the waiter had left and I followed him out into the street feeling heady and daring and glad I'd got through my first year at Trinity.

In so far as she is attractive, a woman is prey to men's desire. Unless she refuses completely because she is determined to remain chaste, the question is at what price and under what circumstances will she yield.

Night had fallen but it was still warm. I felt hot and breathless as if all the air had been sucked out of the city. The man selling flowers outside the Tube looked like the gardener at the convent. I thought for a moment it was him, but it was just the green checks of his flat cap and the tone of his voice. 'Fiver a bunch,' he was shouting. 'Come on, only a fiver. Buy a bunch for the lady.'

Nahume bought a bunch of tulips, which I thought was totally weird and I wondered if perhaps he hadn't taken me for a working girl, just a lonely girl in a red dress looking for a good time.

We got a taxi that drove for about three minutes across Knightsbridge and a man in a grey top hat and tails opened the door for me when we stopped at the hotel. My heels tapped like castanets as I clipped up the steps to the foyer with its thick carpets and minions rushing about with trolleys and bags. Nahume asked for his key, and the girl behind the high desk gave me a condescending look as she handed it to him. I wanted to say, hey, I'm not like that, I'm not what you're thinking. But perhaps Bataille had a point: *By the care she lavishes on her toilet, by the concern she has for her beauty set off by her adornment, a woman regards herself as an object always trying to attract men's attention.*

If that were the case, I'd really hit the big time!

We rose in the lift to the ninth floor. Sweat prickled under my arms. My heart was beating so fast it made my breasts swell out of the dress. There was still time to explain, go back down in the lift, but I bit my lips, followed him into a suite and listened as the door locked behind me.

He took the flowers and placed them on the table. He then stood back and flicked his hand in a gesture that was obvious. This was the moment of truth, the moment when the woman becomes an object, as Bataille had written. I hesitated still and he may have taken that for reluctance, because he removed his wallet from his pocket and counted out £250, which he laid on the table beside the flowers.

'You need help?'

'No,' I said.

My fingers were already thinking for me. I lowered the zip at the back of the dress and stepped out of the material. I unhooked my bra, ran my knickers down my legs and stood there in front of him naked, ashamed, of course, but excited, too. I had never done anything like this before and I thought perhaps Bataille was right, there is in every woman the desire to be an object, the desire to reveal her charms, take the gift.

He walked through to the bedroom and I followed. He threw his jacket over a chair, pulled off his silver tie. He was still wearing his shirt and trousers as he sat on the side of the bed.

'Come.'

I stood in front of him, my knees touching his knees. He ran his hands down my sides, over the curve of my waist, my thighs. I could see lights in the sky through the long window, planes sinking like falling stars as they descended into Heathrow. He kept sliding his hands up

69

and down, up and down. Then he slid his fingers over my tummy and across my ribs. He took my breasts in his palms and squeezed, harder and harder until it hurt and I winced with pain.

'Good, you like. You like. Here. Here.'

He was pulling me sideways. When my legs were locked against his thighs, he bent me forward so that I was suddenly lying across his knees. I can't even be sure how this happened. He started stroking my bottom, gently, like he'd stroked my sides. I stretched my hands flat on the floor and looked down at my red nails through my hair. I opened my legs wider to keep balance and he ran his hand into the crack of my bottom. Sweat was pouring from me. I could feel it under my arms and on my back.

He kept on stroking, stroking. I relaxed. Then, out of the blue, I heard this hard ringing slap. I felt numb and disorientated. My bottom stung and I realised that he'd hit me. One hand was pressing down on my back, holding me still, and he smacked me again. I wriggled like a fish on a line to get away.

'No, don't. Don't. Please don't,' I cried, but he held me still and spanked me again, really hard, the sound vibrating around the room. My head was upside down. I felt dizzy. My throat was dry. I felt ashamed, too, my bottom in the air, my pussy wet, the pain running up my back and down my thighs. I kept wriggling, but he was strong like Andy Masters, and held me still, spanking me again and again.

Tears fell from my eyes. I didn't imagine anything like this was going to happen. I thought we would have sex, I was prepared for that, but this was more intimate, like peeing in front of other people, intimate without being sexy.

Then he stopping slapping me and started stroking me again. I was sobbing, my breasts hanging heavily

70

below me. Then he started smacking me again, not as hard, but continuously, one cheek then the other. My back and thighs were glowing and for some reason I can't explain, it stopped hurting and my whole body was tingling with strange new feelings, shame and guilt and horror, even a weird sort of pleasure I can't describe but it's like being a child and you don't have to think for yourself, you just accept everything.

To my own complete surprise, I was sopping wet. He parted my pussy with his fingertips and pushed his long fingers up inside me, stoking me, in and out, in and out. He gave his fingers a good soaking then pushed them in my bottom, slowly, and it hurt at first but then the pain went away.

'You like, eh?' he asked, and I just sort of shrugged. I couldn't do anything else.

He pushed my legs wider. Then he took hold of my waist, pulled me up and twisted me round in one quick movement so that my toes left the floor and he had his head between my legs. He held my thighs and started licking my pussy, the crack in my cheeks. My bottom was in flames but his moist tongue made the fire go down.

I was standing upside down on my hands, my back straight, my legs bent at an odd angle, Nahume gripping me by the waist so that I didn't lose balance. He was like a piston making me wetter and wetter. My arms were beginning to ache. His tongue was a little animal burrowing so fervently into my pussy something totally humiliating happened. I started to climax. I pushed back and he kept going deeper inside me. I had been crying and now I was yelling, yes, yes, yes. Spasms were vibrating through me and my whole body turned liquid as I erupted in orgasm. I was embarrassed and ashamed, and oddly contented.

He rolled back on the bed. We were a mass of arms and legs. Then he sprang forward to his feet and undressed, dropping his clothes on the floor. He licked his fingers and smoothed back his moustache. There was barely any hair on his body and his cock was long and brown with a shiny purple head. I lay flat on the bedcover and he straddled me, squirming forward. He propped a pillow under my head. I opened my mouth, closed my eyes, and he started to pump in and out of my mouth. My bottom was hurting again, but the rest of me was calm and I kept thinking: I'd have to work a week in Starbucks for £250. He kept going, in and out, my jaw was beginning to ache, then he stiffened, his body shuddered and my throat filled with warm foamy semen that tasted of foreign food and faraway places.

He pulled out and looked into my eyes.

'Camilla,' he said and I nodded guiltily. 'You good girl.'

That was it.

I washed my face, dressed, slid the five red £50 notes into my bag and took my bunch of tulips. He watched, lying across the bed, one hand behind his head, the other combing his pubic hair.

'Here.' He waggled his finger and I approached. There was a notepad and pen on the bedside table. 'You put your number,' he said.

I was about to do so when I remembered Camilla's number, an easy sequence of sevens, fives and threes, and that's what I wrote.

– *Chloë, Cambridge, UK*

Retail Therapy

I've often feared that my insatiable lust for new clothes would land me in trouble, but not this sort of trouble. My favourite fix is a new dress, especially the light summery type, as I feel my very curvaceous backside and hips bring out the best in them; it's the way the hem dances with the wiggle in my walk, I think.

My boyfriend Ryan often gives me a hard time when he discovers a new outfit in the wardrobe or if he sees me sporting a dress he hasn't seen before, but he's a bit of a hypocrite as it's never stopped him fucking me in my new dress or skirt.

During last summer he gave me a little advance notice of a get-together planned by his friends in a nightclub in town, and my usual logic circuits went to work, justifying a new dress for the occasion. Ryan and I don't live together so it's really very easy indeed to find a little space to hit the shops without him knowing, especially if I take an afternoon off work.

It was a beautiful day, quite hot and sunny, but with a strong breeze to cool the skin – and bring out the nipples if you're not careful; many of the girls I saw wandering about town had overlooked that very fact, I noticed, and I allowed myself a smirk at their lack of foresight. I smirked, that is, until I noticed mine were also rather prominent. I had gone with a cropped top, but had chosen one made with a thick blue cotton, thinking that this would allow me to go without a bra, which makes me too hot in the summer. Evidently, the cotton was not thick enough. I hoped they would go down once I got inside the shops.

I always try to avoid the shop assistants, preferring to browse without someone watching over my shoulder. I'm sure everyone is the same. With the shops being so quiet during a working day, it was a little difficult, but by keeping my eyes to the floor and by looking like I knew what I wanted, I managed it. Anyway, left to my own devices I had picked out four possible dresses from my first three shops: they were all on the short summer dress theme, and all patterned with either a floral print or, in the case of one, white dots on navy blue.

My biggest hopes, though, were for the next shop. I can't say which particular chain it was, but it is surely the most popular clothes shop on the high street. Again I kept my head down and set about my business, rummaging through the racks for something sexy. I found a couple of nice things quite quickly, just as I was expecting to, but I pressed on, knowing that there was bound to be something knockout if I kept looking.

I was not expecting to be spoken to and at first I missed the comment from the girl behind me. I asked her to repeat it.

'I wish I had your figure,' she said.

I laughed.

'Oh, thank you,' I replied.

She smiled. I noticed her eyes flick down at my rather too-prominent nipples for a second, and I suddenly felt very self-conscious about them. If girls were glancing at them, heaven knows how much staring I was getting from the guys in town. I thanked my lucky stars there had been no construction work in the main street at that time.

She was small, much smaller and slighter than my voluptuous form, but very well-proportioned in an athletic sense. She had fine blonde hair down to her shoulders and big, very big, blue eyes and I'm sure she was very popular with the lads the way she wore her cropped top displaying her studded belly-button. In fact, looking at her, I found myself wondering exactly why she would express jealousy at my appearance.

'Mind you,' I checked, 'you're much slimmer than me, I don't know what you want my figure for.'

'Thank you,' she said. And jumped. It was just a little jump, on the spot, but it was definitely there. 'But you're much better off than me, you look like a real woman, with those curvy hips and that full bum and that tiny waist by comparison. I'm so, so jealous.'

It was then that I noticed her name badge and realised that I was talking to a shop assistant, apparently going by the name of Debra.

'I would love to help you pick out something to really make the best of your fantastic body. May I? I'm Debra, by the way,' she said, pointing to her badge.

I feared a sales gimmick, but her enthusiasm seemed genuine, so I agreed.

'I'm Amanda,' I answered, 'I'm looking for a summery dress, something that would go well with heeled sandals.'

'Yes, nice. Let me see . . .'

Debra scooted around a few racks, glancing at the garments on the hangers and then at my breasts and my hips, measuring me up. She came back with two dresses.

'I think you should try these on,' she suggested, pointing to the dressing rooms. I followed her.

'It's a shame,' she said, turning to me. 'There was a

crochet dress that would have been perfect for you, but it's sold out. I'm sure you'll look great in these though.'

I took the first dress, a cream-coloured one with a red-orange flower print on it, and I stepped inside the dressing room. I was surprised, however, to hear the curtain closing behind me and further surprised to see that Debra had stepped into the cubicle with me. Not exactly ideal, or even expected, but she was so enthusiastic and helpful, and she took up so little space, that I just shrugged my shoulders and said nothing.

I stripped to my knickers and top, and slipped the dress over my head, allowing it to fall down to my waist. Facing the mirror, I shook the dress down and Debra smoothed out the folds, brushing the dress with her tiny hands, downwards towards the hem. Her fingers tickled my tummy and the tops of my thighs as she did so.

I looked very sexy in it. The hem wafted loosely halfway up my full thighs, and the cut of it accentuated my hips and waist beautifully. The neck was a V-cut and displayed that glistening area of the chest where the roundness of the breasts starts to form.

'Yes,' I laughed, 'I would shag me if I met me in this dress.'

'Me too,' giggled Debra.

'If I was a guy,' I added.

''Course,' she said.

I gave myself a twirl in the mirror, and ran my hands over my hips, smoothing the fabric on my skin. I played on the hem with my fingers – yes, I felt very sexy indeed.

'There's one weakness of the pleated skirt though,' commented Debra. 'It teases, but it hides the full natural mermaid curve down to your thighs. Let's try you with another.'

I nodded and reached down to lift the dress over my head. Debra helped, pulling it over my head. To my surprise, I felt my cropped top also going over my head with the dress. Unable to see, and with my arms trapped in the sleeves of both garments, I could not readjust the top to let it fall back down and Debra was so enthusiastic with her assistance that my initial efforts at resistance were completely overpowered.

I was topless now. Indeed I was nigh-on naked, the only covered flesh was under my lacy ultramarine knickers. I reached for my top. It was strange that such a tight top would come off with such a light dress, I thought. Debra helpfully separated the two for me.

'I wish I had your breasts too, Amanda, they're beautiful,' she observed, admiring my fresh handfuls. 'The perfect size.'

It was not breezy in the shop, but I felt them tighten a little nevertheless, exposed to the air. I half-gestured for the return of the top, but Debra simply put it on the bench where my jeans and shoes lay, and instead handed me the second dress: a very short light-blue stretch design with a horizontal rippled ruche effect. I took it instead, surmising that it would cover me up again just as well.

'So what's the occasion and where is it?' Debra asked as once again she helped me on with the dress, this time smoothing it carefully and tenderly over my hips and onto my thighs. Her hands reminded me of the hands of a lover as they passed over me and I felt warm inside remembering past passions.

'My boyfriend is meeting his mates and their girl-friends for drinks in Bleu on Saturday, you know, the club down by the square. I felt like I needed something new for it – especially if there are going to be girls there I haven't met before.'

'You don't want to be outshone.'

'Exactly,' I agreed, turning to look in the mirror.

77

'Not much chance of that,' said Debra, admiring me with wide eyes.

She was right. If the last dress was sexy, this one was obscene, showing my full form from my breasts down to my thighs, even allowing a hint of the mound of my abdomen curving down towards my sex. Were it not for the contour of the ripples on the dress I would have felt naked.

'Now I *would* shag you,' said Debra.

'Me too,' I said, mimicking with my hands the motions that her hands had made seconds before over my hips and down my thighs. I rubbed the sole of one bare foot over the other and let my legs caress each other at my knees. Being gorgeous was making me feel horny.

'This is the one,' I whispered.

'I agree,' whispered Debra.

I turned to face her and she looked at me again. I exhaled, almost a sigh, as though it might expel my amorousness from my body. I looked back at her. She made the same-sounding breath herself and we stared at each other. Finally, I smiled.

'I'll take it off so you can pack it,' I said.

She helped again as I removed the dress, and I felt her little fingers on my tummy and brushing over the sides of my breasts as she lifted it over my head.

I quickly started to get dressed, hoping she wouldn't notice the small but embarrassing wet spot on my knickers.

'I'll see you at the counter,' she said, collecting the dresses and slipping out through the gap in the curtain.

At the counter I paid for the wonderful dress, and Debra gave me a card with the store number printed on it, along with her name written in hand.

'Let me know how it goes,' she said as I left.

I was itching to get into my dress and out on the town with my horny boyfriend. I also found myself thinking about the experience of buying the dress all week, which had made me feel so sensuous. I even considered doing some more shopping for some matching shoes, but settled for a pair of teal-coloured heeled sandals that I already had, which were almost a match for the blue of the dress.

I decided that the best way to spend Saturday afternoon was to work on the tan on my legs. The sun had his hat on again that day and I was loath to pass up the opportunity for a natural darkened burnish to my pins.

The final effect after a day in the sun was fantastic. My moisturised tanned legs and feet were the perfect complement to the overall outfit – the shoes, the dress, my dark-brown hair and make-up. I was so proud of it all that I rang Ryan to tell him I was running late and that he would have to park the car and come up to the flat to get me. Of course it was just an excuse – I just wanted him to see me posing in the hallway as he came in.

He was blown away as he opened the door to see me standing there, my legs in that mermaid-like pose Debra had talked about, barely covered in the tight blue dress, cut at the thigh. My shapely calves and thighs twinkled with oil and perspiration and thanks, to the heels on my sandals, they were at just the right tension to make them look irresistible.

'Wow,' he said. 'That's fantastic.'

'Thank you.'

'What are my friends and their girlfriends going to think?' he asked with a distant twinkle in his eye.

'They'll know who's boss,' I said, smugly.

There was a moment of wonderful sexual tension as I waited for him to make his move. He said no more but lunged at me and kissed me, grabbing an arse cheek as he pulled me close. I felt one of his fingers brush me just below the anus and I whimpered to feel it as he forced his ardent tongue around my mouth, tasting me.

His finger sought out my groove, rubbing me to wetness through my dress and knickers as his kissing turned to a nibbling on my cheek and then on my ear. I felt a goose-pimpling down my neck. I guess I kind of got the impression then and there that I'd be going out with a pussy full of spunk tonight.

Insistently, but not roughly, he turned me round as he kissed and nibbled my ear and then the back of my neck. I felt my dress being lifted up and my knickers being slipped down a foot or so. He rubbed my lips with a couple of fingers and I reached around behind my head to pull him nearer by the back of his neck, just to show him I approved.

With one arm around me he undid his trousers; the belt jangled as they fell to the floor; and I felt his fine erection brushing between my buttocks. He was full of animal lust and I had no inclination to resist him when he was like this.

He pushed firmly at my wet entrance, squeezing me onto him until I inevitably felt his head pop inside; once he felt the warmth of my walls on his penis there was no holding him and he began to thrust deeper and deeper until my pussy was fully open to him and every lust-filled animal thrust. His hands were all over me, rubbing and squeezing my breasts, playing with my clit, stroking my smooth golden legs, all adding to the enjoyment for me.

I normally have to remind him to hurry up when we're about to go out, but not today. I suspect he had wanted to shoot hot white semen into me the minute he had seen me that evening and getting to climax was the only thing on his mind as he fucked me hard and fast there in the hallway.

'Shoot it, shoot it,' I whispered in encouragement.

He growled, and I knew I had turned him on.

'Come on, right up me, give me your spunk,' I insisted bawdily.

'Yeah,' he growled, fucking me with even more vigour.

I wanted to feel his pulsing cock come inside me and I began again, repeating the mantra. He couldn't take it, he was screaming with pleasure.

I threw my head back with dreamy satisfaction as his cock pounded and twitched, and I felt his seed going into me. I encouraged him to keep going for a few minutes afterwards, but he was breathless and I think the sensations were too much for him and he had to withdraw.

'Well, I don't know if it's safe for me to wear this in public if that's what's going to happen to me,' I joked, straightening myself up in the hallway mirror.

He smiled at me like lovers do.

'Come on, we'll be late,' he said.

His friends did sort of gawp when we got to the pub but no one went so far as to roger me on the spot. I also noticed some deflated and limp handshakes from some of the girlfriends I was introduced to. It just shows you: some of them were prettier than me, but presentation and attitude is so important when it comes down to it. I even noticed the pretty ones nudging elbows into their boyfriends' ribs as a warning not to look at me so much.

After a few drinks and a few dances, though, jealousies were forgotten and we were all getting along fine. I went to the bar on my own for a round – Ryan and I are not one of those dreadful couples who buy a round together – and I took full advantage of the bar top to lean forward and show off the backs of my legs and the contours of my hips and arse. As I waited, and let's face it, looking like this I was unlikely to wait for long, I heard an unexpected voice in my ear.

'Oh, Amanda, you look even fucking sexier than I imagined.'

I turned to see the diminutive figure of Debra from the clothes shop smiling up at me.

'Oh, hello!' I said. I leant forward and gave her a kiss to greet her; she returned the gesture enthusiastically. 'Thank you, I was rather pleased with the overall effect.'

Debra looked me over again, and placed a hand on my waist, tracing the shape of my body through the dress.

'Yes you're amazing,' she said distantly.

'What are you doing here?' I asked. It seemed a better question to ask than: do you come here often?

'Oh, I persuaded some friends to come out here with me. I just had to see how you looked on the night. I hope you don't mind.'

I wasn't at all sure how to take that news at first, but I supposed it was just a friendly and flattering gesture in the end. Her hand continued to rub over my hips and lower back, and the memories of slow relaxed sex with past lovers were revived again, just like they had been in the changing room.

I squeezed over at the bar to allow Debra space to stand with me while I bought drinks.

'You want one?' I asked her.

'Peach schnapps and lemonade please,' she answered.

As we waited for service she continued to check out my outfit. I don't really blame her, she could hardly see over the bar anyway!

'How did you get your legs so tanned and shiny like that?' she asked, noticing my gleaming pins. I looked over my shoulder at them and she reached down to run the back of her fingers on the backs of my thigh.

'Sunbathing and loads of moisturiser,' I giggled.

'Hmm, lovely. So do I get to meet your boyfriend?' she asked.

'Of course, I'm sure he'd love to meet you. He never protests at meeting another pretty girl,' I said.

She giggled her little giggle again as a barman came over at last and took my order. All the while her fingers had continued to feel the backs of my legs and I found myself asking myself if I should move away. I didn't mind her feeling the glossy surface of my skin out of curiosity, but I began to wonder if she was ever going to stop. I didn't want to make a dysfunctional gesture like moving away, which might seem petty or unfriendly of me.

I tried to ignore it, but it was impossible; it felt so pleasant, her tickling me in so sensitive an area. She wasn't for stopping and what I had suspected a little bit the moment I met her, and pondered on a little more as I had got to know her, became clear to me: she fancied me and wanted me.

If her previous touches had not brought me those pleasant sense memories, and if this one had not felt so nice, I would have pulled away immediately. If I had been asked a week ago if I would let a lesbian touch me like this I would have said no way, but now I was here, I was loath to put a stop to it.

I let it continue as I received the drinks on a tray and paid the barman. A nervous feeling began in the pit of my stomach, like the feeling during your first ever kiss and, I don't really know how to describe this, but a pleasant taste seeped into my mouth somehow from the back of my throat. Is that normal? I don't know. My senses were alive and my nerves jangled with the experience. Finally I felt the walls of my vagina moisten.

She stopped, finally, as I picked up the tray and she followed me back to Ryan and his friends. I dished out the bevvies to everyone, including Debra, and as calmly as I could I introduced Ryan to Debra and vice versa. They got on quite well; indeed, there was little space for Debra to sit with us, and she sat on his lap without so much as a word. Ryan took her forwardness very well and we enjoyed a little chat about nothing in particular while she drained her schnapps. Debra took me by the hand.

'Come with me to the toilet, I hate going alone,' she said.

I stood up, and so did she, saying her goodbyes to Ryan and leading me by the hand towards the ladies'.

'I'd better get back to my friends,' she sighed once we had rounded the corner. 'Say, that crochet dress came in this week. I *really* think you should try it, you were made for it. Will you come by in the week?'

I really couldn't resist. She was being so nice for one, and for two, my experiences at the bar were drawing me to her.

'Ryan's quite handsome, but you're prettier,' she whispered, and kissed me, holding it there for longer than she should and longer than I should have let her.

I watched her return to her friends.

I worked extra on Monday and Tuesday to get Wednesday afternoon off for a shopping trip. Those two days were very strange for me; there was no shame or regret, but I felt naughty and even decadent for feeling the feelings that Debra's touches had given me, and I was certainly unsure about what it all meant.

I think it's true that all girls gain some security or comfort from physical contact with each other, but it's never been sexual for me, not even when I dance with my girlfriends in a club – often holding their hands or resting a palm on their hips – both actions that I would consider come-ons if I did them with a guy on the dance floor. But I felt sort of differently about my contacts with Debra.

The trip to the shops itself wasn't much of an expedition; I was only interested in one place. As I arrived Debra was helping another customer in her usual generous style and I casually browsed while I waited for her. I saw her notice me out of the corner of her eye and felt a tingle of nervousness inside, which slowly built up as I wandered around the racks, casually keeping the corner of my eye on her like some store detective.

Before too long, she had served the customer and was beckoning me over with a wiggle of her very feminine hand. I put a blouse I was toying with back on the rack and went to join her. She went directly to the subject at hand:

'Hi. This is it, what do you think?' she asked, showing me a white skimpy tight-looking crochet dress, with its lace-like patterns weaving revealing gaps between and within the designs. It was a little more than I was expecting and I flushed at the idea of wearing it in public.

'Racy,' I gulped.

'But you do racy so well,' she told me, squeezing my arm. I smiled at her like a blushing schoolgirl being asked for her first dance.

'Doesn't it need underwear?' I asked, poking an explorative finger through one of the holes in the pattern.

'You'll have to make do with the underwear you're in – you're not allowed to take underwear into the changing room.'

I had worn white underwear that day, I don't know why, but the decision seemed to have worked out well, whatever the reason. We headed straight for the changing rooms. Again the shop was not so busy and I didn't have to wait for a booth. Again, Debra followed me in.

With the curtain closed behind her, Debra's eyes seemed to change, gleaming a little, perhaps even seeming darker as she looked at me. I smiled again and began to undress to my underwear. I reached out for the dress.

Debra paused before giving it to me, admiring me from my bare feet all the way up, past where my thighs curved into my hips, over my smooth rounded abdomen, to where my breasts squeezed themselves into my bra and heaved in the excitement. I felt her eyes exploring me until finally she handed me the dress.

I wriggled and squirmed my way into it. It was so tight I could feel it influencing my shape, pulling me in around the hips and arse, drawing my thighs together so that I could feel them touch each other, tickling very slightly. My breasts pressed against the fabric and were squeezed to one another, accentuating my cleavage. I turned to the mirror.

Magnificent. How could anyone resist this sight? I looked amazing in this dress and the revealing gaps in the woven pattern were simply turning a raunchy dress into a downright immoral one. I felt good, very good, empowered and sexy, irresistible to anyone.

'Oh, my,' said Debra, biting her finger.

'You like it?' I said jokingly, as I knew full well the answer.

'Oh, yes,' she replied, now sucking her finger and even licking it with her tongue. I wanted her to touch me, like in the club, but felt wrong to say it or admit it.

I watched her watching me for a second or two more,

sucking her finger, and then she reached forward and placed the saliva-covered digit between my lips.

I closed my eyes and licked it as the excitement in my tummy grew and grew. I felt her running her finger around my mouth as I licked, and then, closing my lips around it, I opened my eyes and sucked it while I looked at her. Debra removed it, licking it clean of our intermingled saliva before reaching upward to cup my jaw-line with her soft hand and drawing me nearer to kiss me.

Our lips delicately caressed each other, getting to know each other at first, until I felt her mouth open and I experienced the warm intrusion of a passionate tongue. She kissed me with long deliberate strokes and I allowed each to brush my own tongue as though passion could be tasted by doing so. My fingers were shaking now I think and my mouth tingled with nervousness as she put her free hand around me and pressed my body to her. I rubbed my bare leg against her, feeling the body of a woman in this way for the first time. My dress rose up my leg as I writhed against her.

Debra's hand now roamed up my back and around to my breasts, lightly brushing me all the way – already I was surprised at how tactile my female lover was. She squeezed my breast lightly, as though testing a peach before eating and, through the fabric of the dress and bra, began to apply slightly firmer caresses to my nipple.

'Mm,' I said, unable to form words while our tongues danced. I kissed her more strongly to encourage her and she responded, slipping her fingers over the top of the dress and under my bra to rub my hardening nipple.

I had now forgotten all the inner debates about whether to do this, or what it would all mean to my life afterwards, I was simply living in the moment and savouring it all as the incredibly sensual experience it was.

Debra had forced the dress and bra to one side and withdrew from our wonderful kiss to suck tenderly on my bullet nipple, flicking it now and then with her tongue. Her free hands now meandered, one squeezing and rubbing my arse and the other tickling under the hem of my dress. I felt its fingers spidering at a torturously slow pace up the inside of my thigh. My legs nearly gave way from it all and I felt myself becoming moist.

Now my inner thighs were becoming sensitised, and the tender tickling of their tanned flesh was overloading me and making my pussy hungry. It salivated onto my knickers. Debra did not seem to do anything by half measures; she seemed to spend an age making my nipples tingle almost orgasmically and my thighs endured seemingly endless sensation until they twitched with the slightest touch.

Debra finally broke my sweet torture. I felt her fingers crawling slowly but certainly towards my sex. My knickers started to gravitate downwards under the influence of Debra's expert fingers, and I took a sudden erotic rush as they slowly slipped down my thighs to my knees and then fell to the floor. I was exposed.

I hoped we would not be interrupted and that we could not be heard by customers in adjacent booths or staff out in the shop. That would be bad news indeed for the lovely Debra, who would surely be sacked, but my real concern was that I wanted so much to experience what was to come.

I held her tightly as I felt her finger deftly flap my lips from side to side before slipping between them. I gasped as quietly as I could as I felt the tip of her finger find my entrance and then follow upwards, along the slick part of my pink flesh, to find my clitoris. She rubbed the pussy juice that had collected on her finger into the glowing red button and I tensed with pleasure, biting her ear to stop me from crying out.

She bit my ear in return and, like two lion cubs playing, we munched at each others' ears and lips as she ran her finger in circles on my clit. The pleasure was so intense that I nearly forgot where I was, it didn't seem important any more.

Debra knelt down and I lifted my skirt up, placing one foot on the small bench to allow my legs to open and present her with full access to my pussy. Again she moved in so slowly, torturing me cruelly but at the same time electrifying my senses, rubbing her lips on quivering flesh and licking the tendon on my inner thigh, making it tense up. I clasped my mouth to muffle my moans.

Finally, Debra's yieldingly soft, wet and warm tongue pressed against my bud and began to lick it, sending me into fits. I pressed a hand to the back of her head to encourage her as she worked her tongue into me, pushing the tip of her tongue under the hood with just the right pressure. I heard her making quiet noises of appreciation as she tasted me and I responded with whispers of 'Yes, yes' to show my own approval.

My clitoris became alive as I moved up to another level of pleasure, the first step on the way to orgasm. Was it luck, then, or experience that she chose that moment to make her next move: I felt her searching little fingers opening and then easing into my hole and it was obvious from the angle of entry they were searching for my G-spot.

'Right there,' I whispered as she found it, so she would know to discontinue the search and set up camp right on it.

She was unsympathetic to the idea of easing my G-spot into the fray, immediately curling her fingers up onto it with a quick jerking motion that had me biting my hand to try and stay silent. Her fantastic tongue kept going on my clitoris and I was now at that point when you're just trying to endure the pleasure without passing out!

It seemed like an age that she maintained the stimulation in this way, but was probably more like two minutes or so I imagine; either way I felt my entire pubic region starting to radiate, even my anus tingled – in a stray thought I even wished I had another girl licking that too; a fine thing for a heterosexual girl to imagine, but what had been wrong to me only a week ago, now seemed so, so right.

Debra's four tiny fingers slipped easily inside me now, increasing the intensity with the stretching of my walls. I was only a short step from orgasm. I heard Debra spitting a few times onto her hand before working it into my already soaking pussy. I was now squelching like welly boots down a muddy lane. It was probably louder than my moaning and I prayed no one out there could hear it.

I only realised what Debra was up to when the tugging on my G-spot stopped and I felt her slowly turn her fingers around inside me, so her hand had swivelled one hundred and eighty degrees. She began pushing with short but firm thrusts with all four of her fingers.

I got another shot of adrenaline at the realisation that she was about to fist me, accompanied by a wave of guilty pleasure. With her small hands, she must have felt it was viable even to my untrained pussy. The thought excited me and I knew the moment her hand popped inside I would probably come. I looked down at her as she licked away on my clitoris and unseen, beneath her chin, her knuckles pressed their way into my entrance. I bit my left hand and covered my mouth with my right: it was too much.

Suddenly her hand slipped inside me and yes, I came; I threw my head back and came hard to the sensation of her fist squeezing slowly inside me. Tears of joy ran from my eyes and from my pussy as the fireworks went off.

Debra looked up at me and smiled back at the look of disbelief I was giving her. She continued to squeeze her fist slowly inside me to pleasure me as I came down, kissing my clit a couple of times.

'One of the advantages of being small, is small hands.' She giggled. 'Looks like you'll have to buy that dress,' she added, pointing to my girl-juice on the hem.

'Yes,' I agreed, half wondering if she had got my juice all over it as a sales ploy.

I did buy it of course and I keep that dress for special sexy occasions with Ryan, and to remind me of my experience with Debra in that changing room. Ryan knows all about it now, and I always find he fucks me extra-specially hard when I'm wearing that dress – I bet you anything it's because he's thinking about the time I had sex with another girl, and hoping that, perhaps with him watching on, I would do it again one day.

– *Amanda, Leicestershire, UK*

Bad Boy

I like spanking. Nothing unusual in that, I guess. A lot of people do. The unusual thing about me is that I am lucky enough to have a stunningly gorgeous girlfriend who gets off on spanking me just as much as I get off on being on the receiving end. Like they say, opposites attract. And in this case, I am so glad they did.

I suppose, sometimes I wonder if it's not a bit naughty to get off so hard on being spanked. But that's half the fun, really. Then again, if I'm being naughty, maybe it's a good thing that I'm getting what I deserve, right? My girlfriend, Ella, thinks so. Every time she catches me alone and notices that my cock is hard, she knows what I've been thinking about.

Last night she found me lying on the bed just daydreaming. She said to me, 'Tom, have you been a bad boy?' That's how it always starts. That's all she has to do. If she calls me a 'bad boy' my cock jerks and I know I'm going to do exactly what she says.

'No, ma'am.' I answered, feeling my cock growing stiff in my pants.

Ella is so gorgeous. And even more so when she's feeling strict and bossy. I just can't resist. Last night she was wearing this black lingerie set she has with green and purple shimmery bits on it. Like peacock feathers.

I always call it her Paris underwear, even though it was bought from the local department store.

'I know you're turned on,' Ella said. 'I know you're hard right now.'

'But it's you, ma'am. You're turning me on. I can't help it.'

'That's not the point, Tom.' She strode towards me in her lingerie. 'I ordered you to behave yourself and not spend your time fantasising about kinky sex. Now I am going to have to punish you.'

I jumped up off the bed and sank to my knees in front of her. 'Please, ma'am, no, don't punish me, I promise I'll be good. I'm sorry.' But I don't think she believed a word. My cock was so obviously hard at that moment and I was leaking pre-cum right through my jeans.

She ignored me. 'You will have ten strokes of the paddle for having illicit thoughts about me, and another ten for lying about it. And you will count each stroke out loud and thank me afterwards.'

I looked up at her imploringly. 'Twenty. That's so harsh.'

'Not another word out of place, Tom. Not unless you want your punishment doubled.'

I shivered. I was so turned on by how heartless she was being. And that last threat was enough to keep me very quiet and very hard.

She sat down on the couch by the bedroom window and made me bend over her knee. Ella's a big woman. An Amazonian type. Her lap is spacious and I could actually get quite comfy. My legs were stretched out behind me, with my toes on the floor. My hands were flat on the ground in front for balance. My head was hanging down with my floppy hair spilling over my face, close to her left thigh. I could smell her. I knew how much this turned her on too – easily as much as it did me. I knew she must be wet and sticky with it right now. Hot and open. I could smell how much she liked seeing me submit to her like this.

She raked all my hair up and held it tight in her fist, then used it like a handle to lift my head up and back so I was looking at the bare wall across from the couch.

'Now, Tom, tell me why you're being punished.'

I knew that right now wasn't the time for a smart answer – not unless I wanted to be facing forty strokes instead of twenty – so I said, 'For being a bad boy.'

'A bad boy, how?'

'For thinking about you and getting hard and for lying about it,' I said, my voice faltering a little. She dropped her punishing grip on my hair and let my head fall back down beside her leg. She spent a few moments stroking my arse through my jeans. She always does this. And, as always, I slightly fell for it and started to think that she was going to show a bit of mercy and spank me through the thick denim. So my heart sank when she reached under me for the buttons of my fly.

We were both so turned on we were panting. I couldn't help wondering how long we were going to be able to keep this up.

She used both hands to pull down my jeans. I had gone commando under them, as I often did when I was hoping we would play like this. I know she likes it, likes to find my cock hard and ready for her right under the buttons of my jeans. I am so good to her, really.

Then, before I was ready for it, I felt the wooden paddle against my bare skin and the reality of what was about to happen sank in. For all that I love spanking, I also really kind of hate it.

Ella just stroked me with the paddle at first, but it still took my breath away. I noticed how hard it felt and in a few moments I was panting in her lap, hot, hard and squirming. I couldn't bear it. I was dreading the moment when she started to hit me but at the same time I couldn't wait for it to start. The slow build-up was so excruciating – surely no spanking could be as bad as this waiting?

She took hold of a handful of hair and yanked my head up again. 'Don't forget to count each one, Tom.'

That was normally the signal so I braced myself and then she spanked me with that nasty paddle. The first whack was hard enough to make me jerk in her lap and catch my breath for a moment. I almost, but not quite, forgot to say, 'One.'

She ran her fingers over my flesh again, which wasn't exactly stinging yet, maybe just a little warm. But then, we'd only just begun.

The second stroke followed almost immediately. It was harder than the first, but I was a little more psyched for it too. I said 'Two,' almost calmly.

'Three' and 'four' came a little more quickly. And then my skin was starting to burn quite distinctly. I writhed around and she gave my hair – still bunched in her hand – a warning tug. 'Keep still,' she said, and then delivered an extra hard smack that felt so firm and fast that I was sure she had raised the paddle especially high.

I squirmed, grinding my erection against her lap. 'Five,' I said, my voice cracking. I heard her moan with pleasure. 'Sadistic bitch,' I muttered – just loud enough for her to hear me. Oh, it's bad, I know, but I'm a brat. And when she was this turned on, I knew she couldn't resist a little bit of brattish behaviour.

'Oh, am I really a sadistic bitch?' she said, kind of playfully and paddled me again. 'I ought to warn you, Tommy, that kind of bratty backchat really isn't the way to get me to go easier on you.' She spanked me again. Very hard this time.

I yelled out in pain then said, 'Seven. It's true though, you're such a pervert.'

The spanking got much harder after that little interchange. By about stroke twelve or so I was having real trouble keeping count. Not just because of the burning and throbbing in my arse, but mostly because she kept breaking off from spanking me to stroke my sore skin. And every time she did that she let her fingers dip further and deeper between my legs, stroking my balls, sliding over to graze the root of my hard cock, making me moan and roll and squirm all over the place.

And then I'd completely lost count, but I suspected she had too. I didn't think we were up to twenty, but I knew we were not going to get much further than this. She stood up and pushed me off her lap at the same time. I slid onto the floor and her hands were on me, positioning me on my back, leaning up against the couch. My sore arse burned against the carpet.

Above me then, Ella stepped out of her 'Paris' knickers. She mounted my hard cock and ground down onto it. I cried out as the carpet underneath me started to feel like steel wool as my sore arse moved on it. She tugged at my T-shirt neckline so she could graze her teeth along the sensitive parts of the crook of my neck. I screamed and squirmed.

I was moaning. She was moving hard and fast. God, the way she rode me. It was so hard not to come too quickly. But the last thing I wanted was to go back over her knee for cutting short her fun. Her cunt was kneading me, hot and wet. My arse scraping on the carpet felt like it was on fire.

'Come on, Tom,' she hissed – all danger. She knew how close I was to coming. She wanted to make it difficult for me. 'Don't just lie there and make me do all the work, Tom. Fuck me. Come on.'

I gritted my teeth and looked her right in her flashing eyes. Steeling myself, I lifted my hips and fucked her, driving my cock up over and over into her hot twitching cunt.

She moaned as I moved faster and began to rub herself between her legs.

'Oh God,' I said, bewitched by the sight of her touching herself, turned on from spanking me.

She was panting hard and all she said was, 'More.'

I thrust up harder and faster. I couldn't hold back much longer.

It took nothing more. I started to come and cried out. She moaned when she heard it, not far behind herself. And we both yelled and twisted and fell down onto the carpet, tangled in the clothes we were still half wearing.

Eventually I rolled over and I said, 'So, what happens to me when I'm a good boy?'

– T. Price, Lancaster, UK

Big Yellow Taxi

I spotted her at the corner of Main and Second, frantically waving at me, an anxious smile on her pretty freckled face, braces sparkling in the noonday sun. She was poured long and lean and sunbrowned into a pair of cut-off denim shorts and a white T-shirt, a white mesh cowgirl hat riding her braided blonde hair, a pair of calf-high cowgirl boots on her feet. She looked for all the world like she'd just stepped out of some lonely old cowpoke's wet dream – or the 11:30 bus from Montana.

I sailed right by the pinstriped businessman giving me the pullover salute just ahead of the girl and skidded up to the curb alongside her. She couldn't have been more than eighteen or nineteen, a fresh-faced cutie from ranch country. I was ten years out of Wyoming myself.

As I pushed my big old hack towards the address she'd requested, she told me something about herself. Her name was Cynthia, and she was brand spanking new to the big city, but awful anxious to experience everything it had to offer. Her golden pigtails bobbed around her shoulders as she excitedly chattered away about her dreams and aspirations, her bright blue eyes clear and wide as big sky country.

I got a word in edgewise every now and then as we shunted along the busy city streets and told her something about the city sights, the Checker cab and my own personal history, all the while filling my eyes with the dazzling, sunkissed teenager in the backseat. I sideswiped a couple of cars and three or four pedestrians, staring at the twin points where Cynthia's nipples punched out her tee, and at her long, smooth, crossed legs.

She suddenly jumped forward, crowding the back of the seat right next to me, her slender brown arms folding together. 'You could live in the backseat of this car,' she enthused. 'It's so huge.'

'You can do more than live,' I rasped, the sweet cloying scent of the girl's tangerine body spray, the sunny heat from her nubile body so close and clogging the machinery of my brain. I was forty-five years old, grey streaked my thinning black hair and a hack's spare tire bulged my beltline. I really had no business talking smart to a teenaged hottie. But I couldn't help myself.

'Like ... what else could you do back here?' she asked, staring at my profile, her chin resting on her arms.

Her warm bubblegum breath steamed against my creased sun-burnt neck, causing sweat to roll down the sides of my body in big fat drops.

'Uh, lotsa things.' I gulped and quickly added, 'How 'bout some shade?' The heat inside and out was getting to me. I jerked the big cab over to the right and into an alleyway off Jefferson.

The car rocked to a stop. And after a few breathless moments, Cynthia suddenly touched my damp neck with a scarlet-painted fingernail. I jumped like I'd been cattle-prodded, my head banging off the roof of the cab.

'I bet you could teach me lots of things,' she breathed into my reddened ear, idly trailing her nail up and down my tingling skin. 'About the city ... and other stuff.'

I turned my head to look at her, my neck creaking. Her earnest, innocent face was only inches from mine, her big blue eyes staring at me, her wet, pouty, crimson lips parted. I became so mesmerised I didn't even notice her hand slide down the seat, until it landed in my lap and latched onto my hard cock, uncontrollably tenting my work pants.

I jumped a second time, my body flooding with a shimmering sensual heat, my cock surging in the clutch of the teenager's warm brown hand. I looked down at her hand, then back up into her beaming eyes. Her smiling mouth looked as warm and welcoming as country hospitality. I flipped off the cab's rumbling engine. My own motor was racing flat-out.

Cynthia moved her head closer, her lips brushing, then pressing against my mouth. Her lips were as soft and moist as a dewy spring dawn, her kiss sweet as spring rain. I instantly got thirsty for more, grabbing onto her head and mashing my mouth into her mouth, drinking deep of her youth and freshness, knocking her cowgirl hat right off her head and onto the floor of the sweltering cab.

She squeezed my cock as I ravaged her mouth, the organ growing even harder and bigger in her hand. Warm shivers shot all through my overheated body, as I grabbed onto the girl's pigtails and almost dragged her over the seat with my excitement, hungrily sucking the breath right out of her. I plowed my big old tongue in between her lips and thrashed it around inside the hot wet cauldron of her mouth.

She moaned, her little-girl voice vibrating all through me, her slippery tongue springing to life and tangling with mine. I caught fire, all sense of time and place and fare forgotten. Our tongues entwined over and over, until I finally dropped her bridle pigtails and shoved her backwards. Then I vaulted over the seat and into the back of the car with her, like an overexcited cowpuncher hurtling himself onto a horse and flying right over the other side of the saddle.

I landed with a thump on the floor of the cab, scrambled to my knees and flung myself onto the spacious leather seat next to where she was sprawled. She put a hand to her mouth and giggled. Then moaned, when I reached out my own big, hairy, sweaty hands and grasped her firm titties through her tee.

'Yes!' she squealed, sticking out her chest.

I excitedly felt up her cupcake boobs through the thin cotton, thumbing her sprouted nipples. Then I yanked the shirt out of her shorts and up over her chest, baring her breasts. I went skin-on-skin with the teen's bronzed boobs, grabbing onto the hot, smooth, jelloey mounds and mauling them.

She gasped, shuddered. I pinched her shiny-brown up-thrust nipples and she shook in my hands. I squeezed and kneaded her thrust-out B-cuppers, rolled and pulled on her rubbery buds, until she just couldn't take it anymore.

'I wanna taste you – your cock!' she cried, swooning to her knees on the floor of the cab and clawing at my belt.

I helped her fumble my straining belt open and tug down my fly. Then I arched up off the seat so that she could yank my pants and boxers off. My cock sprang out and slapped my belly, steel-hard and pulsing.

'Have you ever ... sucked a man's cock before, Cynthia?' I gritted.

She stared, wide-eyed, at my jumping dong, biting her lower lip. 'Never ... a real man's before,' she whispered, awe in her voice and eyes. She swallowed hard, then grinned braces-up at me. 'But when in Rome ... right?'

I wagged my noggin up and down, and Cynthia reached out and slid her palm in between my belly and cock and wrapped her slim fingers around my throbbing shaft. I almost carved out a sunroof in the shape of my electrified body, jolted by the hot, tender, exquisite feel of the teenager's bare hand on my bare hard-on.

She pulled my ultra-stiff stiffy up off my stomach, held it upright in her gripping hand. Then tentatively tugged on it. I jerked again, groaned, the girl's heated hand motions turning me molten. She crawled closer in between my splayed, twitching legs, bending her head down and my cock further up. Then she engulfed my bloated cap with her puffy lips.

'Sweet Jesus!' I gasped, grabbing onto her silky pigtails and hanging on for dear life, as she tugged on my cockhead with her warm wet mouth.

She lowered her head further down, taking more of me into her mouth, slick lips sliding down bumpy shaft. I watched in amazement, as she kept dropping and dropping her head, swallowing up my cock, my hood gliding deliciously along the roof of her mouth, her tongue cushioning the boiling underside of my fast-disappearing shaft. She hit the three-quarters mark on my dipstick before gagging and pulling back up again.

Then she started bobbing her pretty little blonde head up and down on my raging prong, shiny lips sucking over the engorged, vein-popped surface, curling my toes in my shoes. She played with my hairy wrinkled-tight sack with her free hand, squeezing balls while she wet-vacced dick, making my legs shake out of control.

I surged with a heavy ominous heat, as the barely-legal hottie sucked harder and faster, pulling enthusiastically on my pecker with her mouth and hand, juggling my balls. I was forced to pull her up by the braided reins before I filled her delightful mouth with more than just dick.

'I wanna fu – make love to you,' I growled.

Cynthia licked my pre-cum off her lips and grinned. Then dropped my spit-slathered cock and tightened sack and climbed up onto the seat next to me. I gallantly helped her shed her short-shorts, the white cotton panties with the little black and white cows on them. Her pussy was shaved bare and slick with moisture.

She sprawled back on the seat and spread her legs, pried her glistening pink lips open to receive my pulsating cock. I half-stood, half-crouched in the cab, positioning myself in between the girl's smooth tanned legs. 'Have you ever . . . gone all the way?' I had to ask, sweating bullets, gripping my pulsing pole.

She looked up at me and smiled shakily, her lips trembling and eyes moist. I swallowed, hard. Then gently probed my mushroomed hood into her shiny, puffed-up petals. She hooked her boots around my waist and jerked me forward, plunging my cock into her pussy.

I was enveloped to the tingling balls in the tight wet sleeve of her cunny. Easy as pie. I gripped the top of the seat on either side of her head and started pumping my hips, fucking the cow-country teen. She moaned and squeezed her titties and twisted her nipples, digging her heels into my rump and spurring me on, the pair of us burning like the bright city lights come nightfall.

I furiously pistoned her oven-hot tunnel, smacking up against her shuddering bum. She dove a hand down onto her button and frantically rubbed, feeling up her boobs, plucking at her nipples. The cab bucked and rocked like the both of us, the alley reverberating with our heated moaning and groaning.

'Jesus H. Christ, I'm gonna come!' I had to howl,

unwilling to slow up and unable to hold back without slowing up.

'Me too!' Cynthia wailed, fingers a blur on her clitty. A dam burst inside the girl, hot sticky juices squirting out from around my wildly pumping shaft, as she shivered with ecstasy.

I bellowed, 'Fuck almighty!' hips flying, fingers digging holes in the leather upholstery, thumping the gushing teenager almost right through the backrest and into the trunk. My balls boiled over and my pussy-milked cock exploded, sizzling cum blasting out of my cap and deep into the screaming girl.

We came together over and over, grizzled old city sticker and innocent young country girl, meter clicking way past the hundred-dollar mark and no one paying the least little mind.

Two weeks later, when I picked Cynthia up for yet another 'ride', there was another girl with her – Eileen, her best friend from home.

'I told Eileen all about how great it was here,' the pretty blonde bubbled, as she and her friend bounded into my cab. 'And she wanted to come right away.' Cynthia grinned at my appraising eyes in the rearview mirror, her braces glinting in the dome light. 'I figured you could show her around the big city – just like you did me.'

Eileen had shiny jet-black hair pulled back in a ponytail, a pale round face fresh and scrubbed. Her chubby curvaceous body strained the seams of the polka-dot dress she was wearing, the tops and more of her snow-white breasts exploding out of the stretched-tight garment.

The contrast between her – dark and pale and overblown – and blonde sunny Cynthia was stunning. I let my eyes ping-pong back and forth between the two girls in the backseat, hardly believing my good fortune. This was worth more than all the tips I'd accumulated in a decade of driving cab. I shifted into gear and punched pedal to metal, sending the big yellow taxi and the girls flying.

I shouted out some landmarks as they sailed by, Eileen and Cynthia hanging onto the seat cushions and watching vehicles and pedestrians dive out of the way, ambulances get passed by, Eileen's glasses reflecting the night city's neon glitter.

Then I charged into my favorite alley on two wheels and slammed on the brakes, screeching to a rocking stop. I flung an arm over the seat and gazed expectantly at Cynthia, ready to vault into the back and ride the pair of teenagers at the first crooked-finger signal from the blonde citified cowgirl.

But she had other ideas, ideas as dirty as the city itself. She put an arm around her friend, pulled her close and kissed the dark-haired girl smack on the lips. And Eileen responded, dishing up some country girl-girl for my amusement – and massive arousal.

I gaped at the two kissing teen dreams, cock rising up in my pants like the flag on my meter. Cynthia's hands traveled up and down Eileen's back as they excitedly smooched, her nails skating over the dowdy dress material, scratching the inflamed surface beneath. Eileen moaned, squeezing the sexy blonde tighter in her arms, her big soft tits pressing hotly into Cynthia's handful boobs.

The two girls let their tongues loose, as naughty girls will, urgently swirling their glistening pink stickers together; fervently french-kissing like it was the most natural thing in the world for two female friends to be doing. In front of one dirty, not-so-old man who watched, rubbing his cock through his pants.

Cynthia pushed Eileen's dress off her shoulders and pulled the garment down, baring the girl's voluptuous nipple-puffed tits. She quickly scooped up and squeezed Eileen's boobs, the soft, thick, creamy-white flesh oozing out from between her grasping brown fingers. Eileen tilted her head back and groaned, ponytail dangling.

'Yeah, feel up her titties, Cynthia! Suck on her titties!' I urged, yanking my zipper down and cock out, fisting.

Cynthia lowered her head and hefted a boob and slapped a fat pink nipple around with her tongue, hands kneading the ample bosoms. She sealed her lips around one of the raven-haired beauty's nipples and sucked on it, pulled on it, bit into and stretched it almost right off the girl's tit.

Eileen jerked on Cynthia's pigtails, her eyelashes fluttering and body trembling. Cynthia bounced her head back and forth between Eileen's boisterous rubbery mounds, licking and sucking and biting, her gleaming mischievous eyes locked on the grinning voyeur in the front seat.

But I could take only so much teasing before staining the upholstery. So I scissored over the seat and piled into the back, the girls yelping with glee. All three of us started shedding our clothes like we were going skinny-dipping in a waterhole back home.

Cynthia ended up buck-naked except for her boots on the bench seat, the totally buff Eileen kneeling in between her legs, gripping the blonde's tanned and toned thighs and digging her tongue into bald pussy.

'Ohmigod, yes, eat me! Eat me!' Cynthia screamed, groping her boobs, rolling her nipples.

I quickly saddled up to Eileen's wagging bottom, smacking the girl's plump, peachy cheeks with my hard-on, setting the heavy flesh to jiggling. Eileen jumped, but kept her head in between Cynthia's legs, licking at the writhing girl's pussy. Cynthia whimpered with each wet drag of the teen's beaded tongue over her buzzing slit, her legs wrapped around Eileen's neck.

I righteously admired the erotic scenery for a moment, spanking Eileen's ass with my cock. Then I grabbed onto the girl's waist and felt around in her dark, springy pussy fur with my swollen cockhead. I found her wet spot and lunged at it, plugging pulsating prick into slick silky cunt.

Eileen moaned into Cynthia's mound, as the horny cabbie with the chariot of fire buried his gearshift. My balls bumpered up against the girl's plush bottom. And I started churning my hips, fucking Eileen from behind, as she drilled into Cynthia with her hardened pink blade of a tongue. We went at it like a well-oiled machine, Eileen and I pumping prime teen pussy, Cynthia urging us on, all three of us and the taxi rocking in rhythm to my frantic thrusting.

The superheated air inside the shunting lovemobile became stifling, dripping with the sweet tangy scent of young woman lust and the sharp spicy smell of mature man sweat. I dug my fingers into Eileen's baby-fat and slammed her rippling ass, really pounding her pussy, my battering-ram cock numb with over-sensation, my body ablaze. Eileen reached up and fondled Cynthia's boobs, earnestly lapping at the bucking blonde's pussy, sucking on swelled-up clit. The obscene sounds of frenzied slurping and sucking and squealing and grunting filled the electrified air.

'Ooooh, I'm coming!' Cynthia shrieked, her dewy young body bucking with orgasm. She desperately clutched Eileen's gripping hands to her tits and ground her squirting pussy into her girlfriend's face.

Just as Eileen was jolted by orgasm, her cock-rocked body shuddering with sexual release. She choked on

Cynthia's hot sticky juices, her glasses fogged up and cum-streaked.

I pumped the gasping quivering girl like a madman, reveling in the wicked sight of the two little angels coming like a pair of dirty little she-devils. Then all the sagging muscles on my sweating body suddenly locked up and I jerked with joy, spurting seasoned white-hot spunk deep into Eileen's sweet cunny.

I drove the teen queens all over town in my big yellow taxi. An experienced city slicker showing the two country girls the sights, and a good time. Helping them adjust to life in the big, bad city. And they drove me wild. Nubile nymphets eager to learn the ways of big city life. Dishing out steamy helpings of sweet country lovin' along the way.

– Kyle, New York City, USA

Meet the Neighbours

It was maybe the fourth or fifth time that our neighbours Paula and Glen had invited us round for a drink and there was no way to refuse without appearing impolite. My husband, Doug, said he didn't mind us meeting up with them. But, because I'd heard rumours about Paula and Glen, I was a little reluctant. However, you can only make so many excuses before it begins to look like you're being rude, so we turned up, as invited, at seven on a Friday night. I told Doug we were only staying for one drink and then I wanted him to 'remember' he was due in at work early the next day. That way we could politely leave at the earliest opportunity.

Paula greeted us at the door wearing the thinnest kimono I'd ever seen. It was criminally short, showing off the lower arc of her buttocks when she turned around. The fabric was so sheer I could see the shape of her stiff nipples and the crinkle of her areolae. Doug couldn't stop ogling her. She laughed as she greeted us and explained that Glen had been keeping her busy in the bedroom and she'd lost all track of time. I said we could always go back home but she wouldn't hear of it. She insisted we were welcome, ushered us into the TV lounge, and then switched on a huge plasma screen before disappearing to 'slip into something *less inde-cent*'.

She'd put what looked like an amateur porn film on the plasma screen. There were three or four naked bodies writhing together and, if the sound hadn't been muted, I'm sure they would have been groaning and making all sorts of sexual noises. I didn't want to watch but the screen kept drawing my attention.

We're not prudes. Doug has a small collection of porn movies that are quite extreme. They show naked couples kissing and touching and I sometimes enjoy watching them with him. But I would never think to put them on for the neighbours' titillation. And this was much stronger than anything I've ever seen in Doug's collection.

A dark-skinned couple were having sex with a blonde in the movie. A long black cock kept pushing into the blonde from behind while she buried her face between the legs of the dark-skinned woman. When the blonde woman in the centre of the screen raised her head to the camera, I saw that it was a home movie. The woman who had been fucking the couple was Paula.

'Are you comfortable being here?' I asked Doug.

'Oh yes,' he said, grinning like an idiot. 'I'm very comfortable.'

I couldn't have moved Doug away from the plasma screen with a forklift truck. The dark-skinned woman had disappeared – probably to hold the camera, I guessed – and Glen had appeared onscreen. Paula was on all fours between the two men with Glen's erection in her mouth and the other man sliding between her legs. I stared at the screen with my mouth wide open.

The real Glen appeared a moment later, laughed when he saw what was on the plasma screen, and then snapped it off. 'How embarrassing,' he said, not looking very embarrassed. 'Paula must have forgotten that was in the player.' He took us through to the kitchen to organise drinks and he and Doug chatted about the weather and the weekend's football while I realised that everything I'd heard about our neighbours was absolutely and totally true.

Glen's a fairly handsome guy. I'd never thought he was anything special until I'd seen him in the homemade porn movie. Now, each time I looked at him, I kept seeing him as though he was naked and pumping back and forth into Paula's face with his thick long cock.

It was worse when Paula joined us in the kitchen. She had changed out of the kimono but I don't think I would have described her change of clothes as *less indecent*. Her skirt was obscenely short and she looked so feminine and desirable I felt like a boy in comparison. Paula's legs are gorgeous and Doug clearly enjoyed the view. Her blouse was open at the neck and showing off a criminal amount of cleavage. It was clear she wasn't wearing a bra under the top and I was painfully aware that she was showing off a tempting amount of flesh.

I was also annoyed that Doug was showing so much interest in her.

'Did you see that movie I'd put on?' Paula asked Doug.

Doug laughed and admitted he had seen it.

Glen said he thought she'd put it on by accident and Paula laughed at him and told him not to be so silly. She grasped Doug's hand and asked him if he could do her a favour. She wanted to edit the movie and burn it to DVD, so she could make a copy for a friend. Doug is a whiz at stuff like that but he glanced at me before replying, as though he was asking if I approved. I couldn't very well say no without looking like a mean bitch. As soon as I'd nodded my consent, Paula dragged Doug out of the kitchen, leaving me alone with Glen.

It's hard to describe the atmosphere. I hadn't gone there feeling horny but the electricity in the air was having a strong effect. I could feel a growing wetness in the crotch of my panties and I couldn't deny that I had a strong desire for Glen.

He said, 'You don't mind Paula stealing Doug for half an hour, do you?'

I said, 'As long as she gives him back when she's finished.'

And we both laughed as though I'd said something suggestive.

Glen explained that he and Paula both enjoyed taking videos of themselves, either alone or with other couples, but neither of them had the expertise to transfer the films to disc. He said whenever they tried to work their way through the various software packages, they'd end up watching the movies, and then getting horny and bonking again instead of doing anything with the movies.

The conversation was fascinating. I asked Glen how come he and Paula were bonking with other couples and he explained they had an open marriage and enjoyed swapping and swinging. He asked if I was worried that Doug was alone with Paula and I said Doug would probably be too engrossed in playing with the software to trouble Paula. But, thinking back to that moment, I'm not sure if I really believed those words.

I was really interested to find out how Glen and Paula got together with other couples and I wanted to find out exactly what they did. I asked dozens of horribly impertinent questions but I think the main thing I wanted to know was something I took a while to get round to asking. After seeing their home movie, I was curious to discover if Glen was as large as he had appeared on the plasma screen or if that had been some sort of trick photography.

He said if I gave him a kiss, he might give me an answer. Which is how, I suppose, we ended up kissing. I hadn't intended to do anything so bold but it just seemed natural to respond to his invitation. I worried briefly that Doug might be upset by what I was doing. But I also knew he was alone with a notoriously promiscuous woman, watching a very explicit movie, and most likely not giving my feelings very much consideration. The idea that Doug might be having fun, and I would be missing out if I refused Glen's offer, made me determined to get as much as I could from the evening.

And so, while Glen kissed me, I allowed him to fondle my boobs through my blouse and I stroked his body. He was surprisingly gentle and considerate, exciting me with the subtlety of his caresses rather than by being forceful or intrusive. I asked him if he thought Doug and Paula might be up to something similar and he laughed and said Paula was probably already naked and sucking Doug inside out.

That image got me wet. I don't often go down on Doug and I felt sure, if Paula offered to do that for him, even if he was really distracted by the editing software, Doug would happily consent. The idea of my husband's erection in Paula's mouth was so shocking it made me very wet and very hot and I responded to Glen with more enthusiasm. When his hands went down from my boobs, cupped my ass and squeezed, I think I was ready to have him then and there.

But I had the image of oral sex in my mind and I was driven by a hunger to taste Glen's cock as well as see it. Breaking our kiss, and trying not to let myself slip from his embrace, I got down on my knees to use my mouth on Glen's erection.

Glen didn't complain. He asked me if I was sure about what I was doing but I didn't bother to reply. I simply unfastened his pants and exposed his long pink cock. It was just as glorious as it had looked on the screen. Glen is much larger than Doug. The end of his erection was a dark and meaty purple and the eye had been leaking pre-cum so it shone in the kitchen light as though it had been lacquered. When his cock was exposed I couldn't resist sliding my tongue against the end and tasting him. Staring up at him from my position on the kitchen floor, I felt wonderfully dirty and very aroused.

'Paula didn't think you'd be up for swapping,' Glen told me, as I worked my mouth around his length. 'She's going to be very surprised when I tell her what we've been doing.'

I shrugged and quietly hoped that Paula was doing something similar for Doug. If he resisted her advances, I knew I would be embarrassed to admit that I had gone down on our neighbour. But even the thought of that sleazy admission made me grow wetter and hornier and hungrier for Glen's cock. I put my entire mouth around him and slurped greedily on his length.

I could have come just from sucking him. Like I said before, I don't often go down on Doug, so I suppose that made the action more exciting. But also, because I was being bold enough to suck my neighbour, and behaving like such an outrageous slut, my libido was soaring. I thought of touching myself, rubbing my clit through my jeans, but I knew, if I did that, I would explode in my pants and the mess would be uncomfortable and embarrassing. Instead I simply savoured the pleasure when Glen's cock spurted repeatedly into my mouth. He gallantly helped me from the floor and then passed me my glass of wine so I could sluice the salty taste of his semen from my tongue.

Five minutes later, Doug and Paula returned to the kitchen and Doug was reminding me that he needed an early night for work the next morning.

When Doug and I got home we were both extremely horny and we went at each other as soon as the front door was shut. After we'd finished fucking I asked Doug if Paula had tried it on with him while he'd been editing her movie. I left the question open, so he could tell me if anything had happened. And I made it clear that I wouldn't be angry or upset if he admitted something had occurred between them. But Doug said Paula hadn't stayed with him while he was doing the movie. She had said she'd needed to keep an eye on something in the kitchen and she'd left him alone while he was editing the movie and burning it to a DVD.

I apologised that his evening had been so dreary and uneventful and I promised him, if we ever got invited back to Glen and Paula's, we'd make sure we stayed for at least two drinks.

– Alice, Glasgow, UK

Going For It

I want to confess to something, but confess isn't really the right word because that makes it sound like I did something wrong, when really I'm proud of it. Better than that, because I've finally achieved something I've wanted to do for years. I've slept with another woman.

I'm sure the world is full of women who think that's no big deal at all, but they probably live in a city and they probably have lots of confidence. I live in a tiny village and I've always had a major shortage of confidence. I've always wanted to sleep with another woman too, at least for as long as I've been aware that I wanted to sleep with anyone. I even remember the first moment I became conscious of my desire, watching a pop video and realising that I found the female dancers sexy, not just sexy the way you know another woman looks good, but personally.

I was very confused at first, feeling that my desire was wrong and that therefore there was something wrong with me. There wasn't anybody I could really talk to, but I could read, and did, until I'd come to realise that however awkward my feelings might be socially they weren't all unusual and certainly weren't wrong, at least not by any rational criteria.

Unfortunately it had to remain a fantasy. Some girls may be brave enough to come out as lesbians within a small community, but not me, while being bisexual is in many ways even less likely to gain acceptance. My single experience from that period doesn't really count, and certainly wasn't satisfying, although it did give me an appetite for more.

Where I live, everybody knows everybody else, anything that happens between anyone goes around in five minutes flat, and woe betide anybody who does anything outside the general bounds of social acceptability. Had I made a pass at another girl and been rejected I'd have been labelled the village dyke and my life would have become unbearable, while if I'd been accepted and our secret had got out, which would be pretty well inevitable, my life would have been even more impossible.

This isn't just supposition either. A few years before, one man, obviously a closet gay or at least bi, had taken up a dare to suck another's cock. He never lived it down, and left the village a couple of months later, although the thing that has struck me as weird is that only the guy doing the sucking suffered, while the one who got sucked didn't. Who can make sense of that?

Anyway, I'm starting to ramble. What happened with me was that I was going out with David Endell at the same time my friend Angie was going out with Robert Dury. Everybody was always going out with everybody else, or had just split up or got back together again or whatever. The whole thing was totally incestuous and still is, but David and Robert were slightly older, both very good-looking and very confident, basically a pair of arrogant little sods, looking back, but at the time I genuinely thought I was in love with David. Maybe I was.

What's for certain is that he was teaching me a lot, and while I lapped it up at the time I can see now that he really took advantage of me. He was a selfish pig, for one thing, and used to love to park up on the cliffs and have me suck his cock, but while he'd put a finger in me he never returned the favour, which I particularly wanted him to do so I could shut my eyes and imagine I was with another girl.

I had actually told myself I would never allow a man to put his cock in my mouth, after first learning about it, as I imagine many women do. David soon put a stop to that, talking me into it with the excuse that everybody did, so I should too. That's fair enough, I suppose, but I bet most men don't do what he liked to, which was to come in my mouth really quickly and then start all over again so that it took ages to make him hard and get him to come a second time.

It was David who took my virginity, in what I suppose is an ordinary enough way, with both of us drunk at a party, when he took me upstairs after a lot of slow dances and basically fucked me. That's all there is to tell, really. It didn't even hurt, because I used to ride maybe, and I didn't cry for my lost innocence or any of the things you read about. If anything I was rather pleased to have got it over with, but at the time it was a big deal, and Robert was particularly jealous because he was having difficulty getting what he wanted out of Angie.

Now I think about it, they probably set the whole thing up, maybe even the special bit. In any case, after that night, Angie and Robert started coming up to the cliffs with us quite often and David was particularly insistent about me blowing him even though they were there. I was more than a little hesitant, and made a bit of a fuss over it, but the truth was that the thought of doing something as intimate as sucking David's cock in front of Angie turned me on far more than the act. So

I 'let him talk me into it' as so many girls do, and had the mind-blowing experience of taking him in my mouth and sucking while she and Robert watched and cuddled in the back. I even swallowed, to which Angie reacted with a mixture of disgust and delight that sent a sexual thrill through me stronger by far than the kick I'd got from sucking David off.

The boys tried to say it was Angie's turn, but she wouldn't do it in her mouth and wanked him off instead, desperately justifying herself by calling them a pair of perverts and all sorts of names even while she was tugging at his cock with her top pulled up to let him get at her boobs. He had a rather nice cock, and if it had been me I would have sucked, but at the time I was more interested in watching the way Angie's breasts moved and wishing I could find an excuse to touch them.

I was given it, not that night, nor the next time, but a couple of weeks later. We'd gone through much the same routine, taking a couple of big bottles of cider up to the cliffs and drinking them while the boys teased us into pulling our tops up, only this time after a bit Robert suggested that I touch Angie. It took a moment for what he was suggesting to sink in, and then both of us were calling him names and telling him not to be disgusting even as I wished I could do exactly what I was protesting I didn't want to. Fortunately the boys kept up the pressure, which gave me the out I so badly needed, allowing me to agree but insisting it was purely for their pleasure. Angie said much the same, and to this day I'm not sure if she meant it or not, but I will never forget the feel of her breasts in my hands as I touched another woman sexually for the first time.

The boys loved it, and were egging us on, which was exactly what I needed. They told us to kiss and we kissed, Angie's mouth a little stiff under mine at first, but soon opening and letting her tongue touch mine, which I'm sure was for real despite her giggling disgust the moment we broke apart. They wanted us to suck each other's tits too, which I did, all the time wanting so badly to take her in my arms and undress her and kiss her all over and, most of all, to lick her pussy and have her lick mine.

I sometimes wonder what would have happened if I'd tried. Probably she'd have freaked out completely, but maybe she'd have responded and we'd have done it there on the back seat of David's car with the boys watching, probably pretending it was just for them even when we made each other come. I didn't, which is probably just as well, because there is no way the boys could have resisted boasting about it to their friends and I'd never have lived it down.

That was that, and what's really annoying is that I'm sure it would have happened again if Angie hadn't found out that Robert was cheating on her with Julie, which is the sort of thing that used to happen endlessly with us, and no doubt does all over the world and has since we first came down from the trees, or before. I stayed with David for another few months, until he went to college up-country, but our relationship didn't survive being apart so much.

My relationship with David marked the end of what I see as my teenage years, by which I mean fumbling about in the backs of cars and not being sure what you want or how to go about getting it, because my next serious partner, nearly a year afterwards, was Colin, ten years older than me and an incomer. He had given up a successful but high-stress city job to buy a pub 'in the middle of nowhere', and to me he seemed completely out of the class of all the men I'd ever met before. I decided I liked him immediately, and made my play before any other greedy cow could get her hooks into him, and that was that. We were married the next year, and for the following three I was blissfully happy and only allowed my desire for another woman to creep into my thoughts very occasionally in the dark hours of the night.

They came back only very gradually. I've read that the body releases chemicals that drive the first hot passion between a man and a woman, which die off after a while to be replaced by different ones that ensure a lasting affection. I don't know how much of that is true, and knowing scientists they'll probably change their minds next week, but I do know that after about three years my marriage with Colin became comfortable and easygoing, but with far less going on in bed than before.

Running a pub is hard work, especially during the tourist season, and in the few years we've had it we'd turned it around from a place where the locals drank and any strangers coming in the door got funny looks to one of the most popular gastronomic pubs in the area. Sex has become something that happens once or twice a week, and is often brief, if intimate in a way I suspect is peculiar to couples who've been together across years. More often than not Colin would come first and I would be left to the solace of my mini-vibrator, which to do him credit he doesn't mind me using at all. When I do, I think of how it would be to make love to another woman, which never fails to give me my climax, but also leaves me feeling a little sad, or it used to.

It was all too easy to see myself going through life without ever experiencing my desire, and so while at first my thoughts were nothing more than pure fantasy I slowly began to wonder if I might not make them real.

I began to surf the net, very tentatively at first, reading messages on the relevant groups and forums but never contributing. It was a strange experience, voyeuristic I suppose, and sometimes a little melancholy, to watch friendships and even relationships being formed all around me, and before long I'd begun to join in.

What I was doing seemed very private, and shameful too, because I knew full well what my ultimate intentions were. I didn't tell Colin, which in turn made me feel guilty, but that didn't stop me. I progressed from swapping messages to going into chatrooms, and also learning netiquette and the possible pitfalls of making virtual relationships real. Then one night in a chatroom on a bisexual forum after several too many brandies I admitted I'd never been to bed with another woman but wanted to and within five minutes I'd been sent a personal message suggesting I meet up, with Laura.

I was suspicious at first, scared even, and extremely careful, making sure she was exactly who she said she was and not some scheming male. She was very patient with me, despite being younger, allowing me to take my time and work up the courage to accept her suggestion. I'd wanted to from the start, but still came close to backing out, always finding excuses, until I finally told myself to stop prevaricating and do it.

She was only about seventy miles away, and lived alone, so her house was the obvious choice, but I had no way of making an excuse to be away for the night, at least not one that wouldn't seem highly suspicious. We chose mine instead, because Colin occasionally went up to see friends in London, and who was to know that Laura wasn't just another customer?

I felt deeply guilty and deeply excited all at the same time, and once everything was set to go I couldn't have stopped myself if I'd wanted to. We talked endlessly on the net as the days ticked by to the one we'd chosen. When Colin left that morning I felt a real bitch, but I was telling myself that it wasn't as if I was being unfaithful with another man, and that I'd only do it once anyway, just to get it out of my head.

All day I was nervous, sure that Colin would come back for some reason, or that I wouldn't get on with Laura after all, but when the time finally came it all seemed completely natural. She looked exactly like her picture, middling height with dark hair, pretty but not particularly sexy-looking, at least by conventional standards. I was horribly nervous for the first few seconds, but she simply took over, leading me first in the conversation and then by the hand to bed.

She guided me from the start, first kissing me, very gently and patiently, until my inhibitions began to melt away, then very slowly starting to touch, not the obvious places men always go for, but the nape of my neck and my cheeks, under my chin and the insides of my wrists, until I was ready to melt and had not so much as a scrap of resistance. She had undressed me completely before she took off so much as a shoe, which felt wonderful, stark naked in her arms and lying on the bed – the spare bed I hasten to add – as I watched her undress in turn.

It wasn't until we'd climbed in under the covers that we did anything really sexual, and even then it was very gradual, working slowly up from stroking and kissing each others' breasts to more intimate exploration and, at last, after maybe an hour of slowly building up each other's excitement, the holy of holies, what I'd wanted to do for so many years, taking turns to go between each other's thighs.

That was the supreme moment for me, when after a last brief hesitation I buried my face in her pussy and began to lick. I masturbated while I did it, just as I had so many times when thinking about what I was now doing, and when my climax came it was quite simply explosive. She'd put a hand on the back of my head, holding me to her, which added a nice touch, and when she came she called out my name.

The rest of that night was spent alternately dozing and making love, touching and kissing without the least inhibition, and bringing each other to climax at least half-a-dozen times apiece. It was everything I'd expected and more, admittedly mainly because of her experience, but I thoroughly enjoyed being the pupil to her teacher.

That was all just two weeks ago, and we've talked endlessly since, both on the net and by phone. I know that despite my promise to myself there will be another time, but even if I knew it would only be one tenth as good as the first I couldn't resist her.

– Vicky, Gloucestershire, UK

Old School

'It's nice, really nice,' I commented, after Todd had ushered me into the large well-appointed living room of his parents' home. I smiled anxiously up at my boy-friend-turned-fiancé.

It *was* a nice place – a huge two-storey red-brick house, with white pillars out front, located in one of the newer, and better, suburbs on the outskirts of town. A far cry from the two-bedroom inner-city apartment my parents called home.

Todd gripped my bare arms, tried to rub the goosebumps out of my skin. Unsuccessfully. 'Hey, there's no reason to be nervous,' he reassured me. 'Mother and Father are going to love you, you'll see. I know Father has a bit of a reputation for being a ... stern man, but that just comes from being a school principal for all those years, and now a successful businessman. He's really a nice guy underneath.'

Father was the president of a company that sold online educational content to schools and colleges. And in the interviews I'd read in the financial magazines, he came across as being a cross between an overachieving Marine Corps drill instructor and an overeducated university professor. This was to be my first time meeting the man, eating dinner in his home, and I was more than a little nervous. Especially since Todd and I planned on announcing our engagement that night.

And it was easy for Todd to say his father was a nice guy. He always gets good grades at the college we both attend, is a star in two sports and a class president, editor of the engineering newspaper. A real All-American, apple-pie student success story. What father wouldn't be proud? While my grades are dubious, my achievements and background not so impressive.

Mind you, one of the reasons I'd fallen for the guy in the first place was because of all that wholesomeness and all those accomplishments – plus that golden head of fine blond hair, those bright-blue eyes, and that rock-hard body and bum. He lightly goosed my butt as we hugged each other in that intimidatingly large and tasteful living room.

'Hey, watchit, you!' I yelped, scooching out of his grasp. I grinned at him. Then struck a pose in my high heels, tossing my long dark hair back. 'You behave yourself now,' I admonished. 'There won't be any of that foolishness 'til we're married.' My parents were poor, but they were strict.

Todd laughed, grabbing me in his strong arms and kissing me. 'Which is why we need to get married as soon as possible,' he said, leaving my tingling lips and bussing my nose. I could feel his pent-up need bulging against my belly.

'Show me the rest of the house,' I said, breaking free and wandering off down a lushly carpeted hallway.

He gave me the grand tour. And I do mean *grand*: swimming pool and barbecue pit in the big well-groomed backyard; full-scale wood-paneled recreation room, complete with billiards table, dart boards, and oversized entertainment unit, in the basement; spacious, stainless-steel and black and white-tiled kitchen in perfect order; and two downstairs and three upstairs bedrooms decorated in the very best of taste. Plus three roomy, sparkling bathrooms.

The whole layout was large enough to be called an apartment block back in my old neighbourhood, though nobody would've been able to afford the rent. My anxiety level at meeting Father and Mother, the creators and maintainers of all this, increased with every room we went through.

So that by the time we finally entered the upstairs 'master' bedroom, my little brown body was full-out quaking with qualm. I stared at the brass-railed bed, the picture of the iron-grey man and his adoring wife hanging on the red and gold wallpaper above, the massive polished-oak antique dresser in the corner.

'N-nice,' I mumbled, rubbing my arms with icy hands and wondering why I'd worn only a thin blue summer dress – even if it was ninety degrees outside. 'Well, um, thanks for the tour, Todd.'

'You haven't seen my room yet,' he responded, a salacious grin that still somehow looked angelic on his honest, open face. He turned and walked out, expecting me to follow.

But I lingered, drawn to that gleaming, glowering dresser for some reason. What, if any, intimate secrets did it hold, I wondered? Maybe something that showed the softer side of the hardman who owned the house?

I pulled the top drawer open. I pulled hard, expecting the heavy wood to stick. But it slid out with oiled efficiency, revealing women's underwear, white and cotton and conservative.

I pulled the second drawer open. It was full of men's undershirts and underpants, white and cotton and conservative.

Third drawer: men's socks on one side, women's

stockings and pantyhose on the other. Everything neatly folded and arranged, like in the other two drawers.

Todd yelled at me to shake a leg. I tried to pull the bottom drawer open. But this one stuck. I pulled harder. The drawer grated, jumped, shot open, spilling me backwards onto the blond shag and exposing an imposing collection of straps, paddles, switches, yard-sticks . . . and whips. Piled up in random disorder.

I got up off the floor, hardly believing my eyes. Then I bent down and picked a strap up out of the drawer, just to make sure it was real. It was real, all right – a foot-long, three-inch-wide, quarter-inch-thick slab of black pebbled flexible leather.

I held it in my hand, feeling its heft and texture. Smacked my palm with it, and felt its toughness. I slapped my open hand again, and again, the paler skin of my palm heating up quickly.

Then I caught a glimpse of myself in the big antique mirror mounted above the dresser – little ol' me holding the ominous old-school disciplinary device. My face burned and my body flooded with warmth, the goosebumps gone from my arms. I was getting to know Father a whole lot better.

'Hey, what's the hold-up?'

I almost jumped out of my shimmering skin.

Todd looked at my glowing reflection in the mirror, the strap dangling dangerously from my hand. 'Uh, where did you get that?' he asked, the nervous one now.

He walked over to me and looked down at the open drawer. 'Oh, yeah, that junk – relics from Father's days as a school principal.' He lightly tapped my bum. 'Too bad, too. They might've motivated you to get better grades.'

'Think so?' I breathed, the spot on my butt cheek where his hand had landed tingling wickedly. I didn't bother informing the guy that one of the bamboo switch 'relics' still had its price tag attached. Instead, I smacked my booty with the leather strap, across both cheeks, setting my whole bottom and body to tingling.

The grin faded from Todd's lips as he looked at me in the mirror in surprise. As I whacked my well-packed butt again, harder this time, I bit my lip, quivering – with excitement, not fear any more – watching myself in the mirror: the fixed stare and flared nostrils, the hard thick points poking through my bra and dress.

And when I struck my bum with the strap a third time, really hard, I jumped on impact, my pussy dousing wet in my white cotton conservative panties. 'Spank me!' I hissed at Todd. 'Punish me for my poor grades – all my other failings!'

He stared at me, eyes wide and mouth hanging open. I spun around and grabbed his hand and slapped the strap down into his open palm. 'Spank me!' I repeated, in-control and out-of-control.

I can't fully explain what came over me. A combination of my high anxiety and the couple of drinks I'd stolen out of the flask in my bag (to calm my nerves), maybe, added together with the wild thrill that had unexpectedly rocked me to the core when I'd whacked my own behind, the thrill of sexual discovery. But whatever the cause, what had come over me had come hard and fast and overwhelming. And my astonished fiancé, looking into my glaring, reflected eyes, just knew he had to go along with it.

I turned back to the dresser and placed my hands down on the lace-covered top, spreading my legs and pushing my butt out, digging my heels into the shag. Todd stepped forward and slapped my bum with the strap. Weakly, limply.

'Harder!' I gritted.

He smacked my trembling right cheek. My left.

129

Harder. He moved closer alongside me and laid the leather right across both mounded butt cheeks at once. The dresser shuddered in my hands, shivers racing up and down my spine.

Todd landed another blow on my bottom. And another. And another, the sharp cracking sound filling my ears, the savage biting sting filling my body.

A heavy smash burned my butt flesh. Then shimmered all through me. Then dissipated. Before bursting against me again, the soul-shattering sensations repeating, amplifying, the harsh leather landing harder and faster, until the fiery sting never fully left my battered tail, the blows coming too rapidly now.

I tore my glazed eyes away from the panting, perspiring girl in the shivering glass and looked back at Todd. His face was red, his normally neatly-combed hair disheveled, a look of fixed intensity in his blazing blue eyes. He was destroying my ass with the whistling strap, throwing everything he had into every lash, a crazy grin cutting across his handsome face.

'My dress!' I shrieked. 'Push it up! No, take it off!' I was on fire, ablaze with pain and pleasure.

Todd fumbled the zipper on the back of my dress down, and I shoved the inhibiting garment away from my shoulders, let it drop. Then I unhooked and flung my bra aside, as Todd tore my panties apart.

'Jesus, yes!' I cried, the singing strap landing like a hammer blow directly on the bare skin of my naked butt. The pain was so much more intense, so much more pleasurable.

Todd whaled my bare bottom, the vicious crack of hard unyielding leather against soft yielding skin resounding like gunshots in the sweltering bedroom. Blow after blow rained down on my brutally inflamed bum, sending me arching to my toes, body and brain crackling with eroticism. I blinked a storm of hot tears out of my eyes, pussy weeping into the carpet.

Then Todd suddenly ceased his onslaught, and gathered me into his arms. I quivered wildly against him, his strong arms unable to control the wicked tremors, the echoes of the brutal blows reverberating all through me. He desperately rubbed my bum, his damp hands doing nothing to quench the flaming skin. 'I didn't mean to hurt you! I didn't mean to hurt you!' he kept foolishly repeating, holding me tight.

'Rub my pussy!' I grated. 'With the strap!'

I was primed, stoked, battered to the very edge of awful sexual awareness, and total release, so that when Todd finally rubbed the warm leather edge in between my trembling legs, I exploded in his arms. 'Jesus!' I screamed, erupting with a raw savage intensity I'd never experienced before.

Todd jerked the strap away and replaced it with his hand, rubbing my clit with his fingers, smacking my blistered behind with the leather again, bringing me off with multiple, merciless orgasms.

It was tough sitting through dinner with Todd's parents (literally). But I kept up my end pretty well. They were pleasant, interesting people, happy to hear about our engagement; Todd's father obviously a different person in the warm bosom of his home and family.

And when I was helping Todd's mother clear away the dishes afterwards, and told her how nervous I'd been about meeting her husband, that's when I got my second shock of the day. Because she replied, 'Oh, Chuck can be intimidating at times, I suppose. But when we go upstairs, I'll show you my "secrets" for keeping a husband in line.'

– *Jessica, Boston MA, USA*

Accidental Dogging

I'd been feeling horny all evening but hadn't been able to do anything about it. We'd been visiting ultra-straight friends for a dull evening celebrating their fifteenth wedding anniversary. The party might have been fun if there had been a little more music, and if the people there hadn't been so boring. I'd flirted with a couple of guys but the atmosphere was so repressed I'd known nothing naughty was going to happen. We left early – I think we were the first to leave – and that was only because I whispered to Nick that I was desperate to be fucked. As soon as I said those magic words to him he ushered us to say goodnight to our hosts and then bundled me off into the car.

I wanted to go down on him while he was driving but the steering wheel kept getting in the way. He was hard, and I was enjoying the sensation of having his thick hot cock in my small cool hand. But I wanted him in my mouth – as well as some of my other places. Yet every time I tried to get my mouth close to his groin he would have to turn a corner and the steering wheel would drag against my ear and the side of my face and the nuisance of it all would spoil the moment and sour my mood.

Nick suggested parking at the side of the road but we were still in the suburbs. Although it was late there was a chance a passing pedestrian would see what we were doing and neither of us fancied the embarrassment of a public indecency charge. I had my skirt hitched up, my knickers pulled to one side, and two fingers inside my pussy. I'd been juicy and hot throughout the evening but the frustration of our situation was making my need to come unbearable. When I told Nick to find somewhere discreet for us to park he said he knew 'the ideal spot' and took us out of the suburbs to an area I didn't recognise. When he killed the engine I didn't bother trying to see where we were. I just bent over his cock and got my first chance of the evening to properly suck on him.

It was arousing. It was just what I needed after listening to so many boring conversations throughout such a dull and uneventful evening. I had one hand wrapped around the base of Nick's erection and my other was pressed against my pussy. With two fingers inside I was able to drag my thumb against my clit while I sucked on Nick. I figured: if I didn't make myself come, Nick could go down on me once I'd taken his load in my mouth. I also thought there might be a chance of sucking him off and then sucking him hard again so he could pound me for ages until I was good and satisfied. The idea of being taken over the bonnet in the cold night's darkness was desperately arousing and I wondered if Nick might be up for that.

He came fairly quickly.

I can always tell when Nick's going to spurt in my mouth. His cock gets much stiffer and his balls go really tight. Even if he wasn't closing his eyes and groaning, and saying, 'I'm going to come! I'm going to come!' I'd have known he was on the verge of his climax. So I kept my mouth around him and savoured the sensation of his cock pulsing and his semen splashing against the back of my throat. Once he'd finished spurting I let his cock slide from my mouth and then pushed my face over his.

Nick loves it when I spit his come back into his mouth. I usually pass it back to him with a deep french kiss. It's quite an erotic sensation to have our tongues lubricated by his thick spunk while we kiss. It always gets me horny and I've known it bring Nick back to a state of full erection even after he's just spurted. Nick had his head back against the restraint, his mouth was open, and I was just about to let his semen slip from my mouth and into his, when someone flashed a torch into the car.

I almost screamed.

A man stood outside the car window. From the little I could see behind the bright light he was giving me the thumbs up and had clearly approved of the job I'd done on Nick. When I shielded my eyes against the bright light I could see that there wasn't just one man outside: there were about half a dozen of them.

Nick sheepishly explained that he'd brought us to the local dogging site. He said he hadn't expected there to be anyone there on a Thursday. The usual nights, he said, were Saturdays and Sundays. I wanted to know how he knew so much about the local dogging site and why he had never told me about it. He just shrugged and gave some bullshit excuse about how he'd heard about it from friends. The way he said it made me certain he was keeping something secret. And, while I was pretty pissed off that he'd put me in such a situation, I was also very pissed off because I knew he was lying.

But I was also still very horny.

The guy outside the car kept flashing his torch at me and then pointing at his crotch. I understood what he wanted but I needed to sort things out with Nick before anything else happened.

134

So I asked Nick if he knew about the site because he'd been dogging, and he admitted he had. I asked him why he hadn't told me about it and he eventually said he had just kept it secret because he thought I would have been upset if I'd discovered he'd been there and been blown by a stranger.

I thought about this for a moment, not sure if I was more angry or more horny. It was only when the guy outside the car knocked on the window again that I realised what I needed to do. I was leaning across Nick and my face was on the same level as the stranger's crotch.

As I wound the window down Nick asked, 'What the hell are you doing?'

I said, 'I'm going to suck this guy off while you make me come.'

I could see he wasn't happy about it, but I was past caring. All his arguments seemed to flash behind his eyes before he realised I would have to answer for them. They died away before he bothered to say them aloud. Perhaps he didn't like the idea of his wife sucking strangers at a dogging site, but he was beginning to understand his wife wasn't wholly happy about him being sucked by strangers either – at least, not when it was kept secret from her. If it was OK for him to visit a dogging site and get his rocks off, I thought it should be equally OK for me to do the same thing.

Which was how I ended up stretched across my husband as I sucked on a stranger's cock.

The situation was extremely arousing. I felt as though I was in absolute control. Nick said he wasn't comfortable with what was happening. I told him, if he didn't stop whining, and didn't start trying to satisfy me, I'd make the stranger come in my mouth and then I'd spit the come into Nick's face.

Straight away, Nick's hands were on my pussy and he was teasing my clit and sliding his fingers in and out. I could hear the noisy slurp of my pussy as I sucked on the stranger's cock and worked my lips up and down him. And I could feel that Nick was hard again, aroused either by the sight of me sucking a stranger's cock, or horny at the thought of me spitting another man's come in his face.

It was a thrilling experience for me.

The taste of the first stranger was unreal. His cock was lovely and sweaty. I hadn't expected him to come in my mouth and I wasn't prepared when he finally spurted. I can tell when my husband is going to come in my mouth but this was a different erection and I wasn't used to the telltale signs. I almost gagged when he started to shoot and shoot and shoot. I tried to cough out the come from my mouth but there was so much I just ended up swallowing most of it while the rest dribbled down my chin. I pulled my head back into the car and looked at Nick while half the stranger's spunk was still rolling over my lips.

Without thinking about it we both kissed.

His hand worked more furiously against my clit and he pushed his fingers more quickly in and out of my pussy. When we eventually stopped kissing I pushed my head out of the car's window and said, 'Who's next?'

Within seconds there was another hard cock waiting for me.

I took a moment to admire this one. It was hard and swollen with no trace of a foreskin. Since marrying Nick I'd forgotten how sexy a circumcised cock can look and I fell on it hungrily. Nick was still fingering my pussy and I was getting close to finally coming. If I'd taken a moment to remind myself that I was in a semi-public place, with a stranger's cock in my mouth and my husband's fingers up my pussy, I think I would have orgasmed instantaneously. Instead, because I was concentrating on making sure I properly pleasured the circumcised cock, I simply rode a steady wave of satisfaction that wasn't quite orgasmic – but was close enough for my mood at that moment.

Nick unfastened my blouse and bra and let my boobs hang out. A couple of the strangers outside reached inside and my nipples were rudely fondled and tweaked by men I didn't know. They weren't very adept at fondling breasts but they made up for their lack of finesse with a genuine enthusiasm. Nick continued to rub at my clit and finger-fuck my pussy and I don't know how I avoided having an orgasm with so much stimulation.

I sucked six cocks that evening – seven if you count Nick's – and I kissed my husband deeply after each one had spurted in my mouth. A couple of the guys said they wanted to fuck me, and I was sorely tempted to let them. But I hadn't brought any condoms and it wasn't something I'd talked over with Nick. Even though I was desperate to be fucked – and the idea of getting ridden by stranger after stranger was really appealing – I was content to simply suck the strangers while my husband fingered me and the other strangers fondled me.

I also got a huge thrill each time I rewarded my husband with a wet spunk-flavoured kiss. Nick's erection seemed to grow harder with every kiss and my need for him kept swelling into a desire that was close to being phenomenal.

When we got home I was desperate to come. Nick still seemed upset that I'd gone to such extremes to prove I was upset about his dogging but he was also rock-hard. He explained later that he'd been hard since I took the first stranger's cock in my mouth.

I told him I knew, and that was why I'd continued.

We must have fucked for an hour before he came again and, by that time, he'd made sure I was completely satisfied. Before we fell asleep, Nick promised he wouldn't go to the dogging site ever again. I told him he could go there if he wanted – but he had to make sure I was always with him.

– Barbara, Harrogate, UK

Beth's Friend

The thing was, I'd always felt comfortable around Beth. She was my best friend through primary school and secondary school and we'd both worked at the same branch of McDonald's for a few months until Beth got bored with the place. She was my chief bridesmaid (when I got married to Steve) so we both felt relaxed and extremely comfortable with each other. When Steve said he'd always fancied trying a threeway, Beth was the first person who sprang to my mind.

I didn't believe he was serious at first. I said to him, 'You're kidding aren't you? The idea of a threeway doesn't really turn you on, does it?'

He grabbed hold of my wrist and guided my hand towards his groin. When my fingers found the hard shape of his erection he laughed and said, 'How's that for proof? Can't you tell I'm not kidding when I say it really turns me on?'

I never mentioned anything about my plans for Beth to Steve. I didn't want to raise his hopes or say something that would later turn out to be embarrassing if Beth vetoed the idea. I just told him I was off to visit Beth one Saturday when we were having our weekly girls' night at hers with a bottle of wine in front of a DVD.

I have to admit, I was nervous going round there. I had dressed in some of my sexiest gear, figuring that it usually worked to arouse Steve, so it ought to have the same effect on Beth. Usually I go to Beth's wearing jeans and a jumper but that evening I wore heels, fishnets, a leather mini and a matching basque. It was Beth's turn to supply the wine but I took an extra bottle because I figured a couple of extra glasses might help us both lose our inhibitions.

And it wasn't that hard to bring the conversation round to sex.

Beth was between boyfriends and she seemed to be obsessing about the fact that she wasn't getting any sex. When I talked about Steve she kept telling me how lucky I was to have a bloke and asking how often we did it, and wanting to know whether or not he was any good. A part of me was tempted to just say, 'Why don't you come round to ours now? I'm sure Steve will give you a demonstration.' But, instead, I held my tongue and simply answered her questions as honestly as I could. I told her Steve was an OK husband. I didn't have to fake too many orgasms. And he usually tried his best to satisfy me.

We'd gone through the first bottle, and were halfway through the movie when Beth first noticed my clothes. She commented on the outfit and asked if I was going somewhere after we'd watched the film. Thinking quick, I said I was dressed at my slutty best so I could excite Steve when I got home. Beth called me a lucky bitch and then said she would probably have a man in her life if she looked as good in stockings and heels as I did. She seemed pretty low and I tried to assure her that she had always been the looker when we used to go out clubbing together. But the words didn't have much effect and she seemed on the verge of sliding into a real downer. To prove my point, and to cheer her up, I insisted she should go and change into some sexy gear. After a small protest, Beth disappeared into the bedroom to get changed.

She came back looking sensational.

Wearing thigh-length boots and an ice-white mini-dress I'd never seen before, she looked like she'd stepped off the cover of a lads' magazine. She's got large boobs and they looked like they were almost ready to spill out from the plunging neckline. I was being honest when I said, 'Wow!' But Beth didn't seem to believe my praise was genuine.

'See,' she said miserably. 'I don't look anywhere near as good as you.'

I told her she looked really good but Beth wouldn't hear it. She was drunk and maudlin and kept saying that she couldn't get a bloke because she couldn't turn guys on.

'You're talking nonsense,' I said. 'I'm not even a guy, but you're turning me on.'

I hadn't expected to say anything so bold. And, as soon as I said the words, I felt the atmosphere in the room change. Beth stopped looking miserable and studied me warily. I could feel myself getting short of breath and my clothes seemed suddenly too tight. The basque was pressing against my breasts as my nipples grew hard. My panties felt uncomfortable against the swollen lips of my pussy.

'You're just saying that,' Beth sniffed unhappily. She sat down next to me and said, 'You're not really turned on.'

I grabbed hold of her wrist and guided her hand towards my groin. Parting my legs slightly, pushing her fingers towards the sodden crotch of my panties, I laughed and said, 'How's that for proof? Can't you tell I'm not kidding when I say it really turns me on?'

141

I think we were both fairly shocked by my boldness. And I think it could have been the end to our friendship if Beth had pulled her hand away and acted as though she was repulsed. But, instead of pulling away, she kept her fingers pressed firmly against the crotch of my panties. Even when I let my hand fall away from her wrist, her fingers remained – pressing tight against the wet fabric and forcing the gentlest pressure on the lips of my pussy.

We were watching each other, both wide-eyed and suddenly sober.

Beth said, 'God! I want you.'

I said, 'I want you too.'

And then we were both kissing while Beth's fingers squirmed lightly against the sodden centre of my panties.

The kiss was surprisingly erotic.

Steve had talked about how much he wanted to see me kissing another woman and the fantasy had always turned me on. But I had never imagined it could be so powerfully exciting. Beth's tongue slid into my mouth. I could taste the wine she'd been drinking as she pressed her face close to mine. And I could feel her delicate feminine body as she enthusiastically pushed herself against me. Her fingers pushed at the crotch of my panties and my pussy grew warmer and wetter. When she began to tease the panel of fabric to one side, and her soft fingers stroked my bare flesh, I almost came on the spot. The inner muscles of my pussy clenched vigorously, as though it was desperate to take her whole hand and devour her.

'We're only doing this the once,' she whispered.

I nodded eagerly. I didn't care whether we did it once or a million times. I just wanted her to do it to help release my craving for her. 'Just this once,' I agreed.

'And that's only because we're both pissed and we probably won't remember it in the morning.'

She laughed at that and shook her head and said, 'Don't be so sure. I'm going to make sure you remember this in the morning.'

And that was when she slid her fingers into my pussy. I howled.

Steve has kissed and fingered me before. And I love him and we have the special pleasure that comes from making love rather than having sex. But this was my platonic girlfriend fingering my pussy and I was thrilled beyond anything I'd ever known. I'd never done anything so outrageous in my entire life. The thrill of kissing Beth and being fingered by her was phenomenal. I knew she was going to make the experience memorable and I knew I was going to do my best to return the compliment and make it memorable for her when I got the chance.

I peeled away Beth's mini-dress and marvelled at her body. We've been swimming in the past. We've stayed at each other's house and seen each other naked before so I had no need to leer at her nudity. Yet, when I was confronted by her naked body that night, the unexpected arousal that shook through me was enormous.

Naked, Beth fingered me to a climax.

We continued kissing, and her bare body kept brushing against me. But I remained clothed and she didn't even take my panties off for that first orgasm. She simply kept the crotch of my panties pushed to one side and slid her fingers in and out with increasing speed.

I'd howled when she first pushed her fingers into me. I screamed when the orgasm came.

Beth kissed me through my climax and then I was clutching at her and saying I needed to do the same for her. I knelt astride her, moving my kisses from her face

143

to her huge boobs. I sucked on her nipples until she was sobbing with pleasure and then I moved my head carefully down to her pussy.

I have to admit I was a bit nervous about what I was doing. I'd had fantasies about going down on a woman but those fantasies had never been acted on. And now I was with my naked best friend and on the verge of licking her cunt.

Beth said I didn't have to do anything I didn't want to do, and that consideration only made me more determined to give her pleasure. I pushed my nose through the ginger curls of her pubic bush, and then I pushed my tongue against the wet centre of her pussy.

Beth gasped.

The sensation of hearing her pleasure was so exciting I almost came from simply tonguing her. Whatever hesitancy had made me guarded was forgotten after I got my first taste of her wetness. The flavour was like warm honey, not quite as sweet, but certainly as satisfying. I knelt on the floor in front of Beth, held her thighs apart with my hands, and pushed my tongue deep into her sex.

I occasionally flicked my tongue against her clit.

She was wholly aroused and her clit had swollen up like a small cock. But it was while my tongue was sliding in and out of her pussy that she came. I had my nose pressed above her clit, my upper lip was rubbing against its thrust, and my tongue was pushing in and out between her tight wet lips.

She spurted a mist of sticky wetness into my mouth when she orgasmed. I swallowed it with the same enthusiasm I have for taking Steve's semen. Beth was still shivering with pleasure when she took control of what was happening, forced me to lie down, and then licked me to another climax.

We spent the next two hours swapping positions like that before I realised how late it was. I told Beth that Steve was going to be worried. She looked a little sad but said it was only right that I should go back home to my husband. I phoned Steve and said I'd had too much to drink and would be staying overnight at Beth's.

It wasn't unusual. It had happened before. But this was the first time I stayed over at Beth's and we went to bed to lick each other to climax after climax.

I didn't get round to mentioning Steve's desire for a threesome that night. Nor did I manage it on the next girls' night in that me and Beth enjoyed a week later – even though that was an equally sexual episode. Being honest, I haven't mentioned it to her over the past six months, even though we've been fucking each week and sex has been our main topic of conversation as well as our main activity. But I do intend to mention Steve's fantasy to Beth, and I'm sure he's going to enjoy playing with Beth – just as soon as I've finished enjoying her first.

– *Karen, London, UK*

Susan's Housemaid

After my divorce came through I took the decision to find full-time employment; a couple of months on meagre maintenance payments and my part-time wage from the council convinced me of that. The local government could not offer me an increase in hours, so I had to look further afield to fill my day and my purse.

I did not really have the luxury of being choosy, and I was more or less cornered into taking the first offer that came along. That offer happened to come from the retail sector, specifically a small but successful business in West London called Secret Love.

I had no qualms about applying for a job in a lingerie shop, even with the daring and racy display in the window, which I am sure caused no little controversy in the neighbourhood. The left-hand half of the window was the usual attractive, sexy, but generally tasteful array of basques, nightdresses and stockings you would expect to see, but the window on the right-hand side was a little 'off the wall', containing a display of two female dummies in a more risqué pose: the first was dressed in stockings, suspenders, knickers, a bra, a mortar board and a headmistress's gown. She was sitting down on a wooden chair with her hand raised, and open-palmed. The second dummy was dressed in a school uniform, complete with tie and pig-tails and accessorised of course, with hold-ups and Oxford pumps. She was draped over the knee of the first dummy and no doubt anticipating the receipt of a stinging and traditional admonishment! An eyebrow-raiser if ever there was one, and possibly a distraction from the 'Full-Time Sales Assistant Required' poster that was stuck to the small blackboard behind them.

I phoned for an application form when I got home and, once I had completed it, took it down to hand it in personally. The woman behind the counter was utterly beautiful and I hoped that she had not noticed me turning green at the sight of her. She was in her late twenties, like me, and had the purest smooth white skin and bushy curly black hair – mostly scrunched on top of her head, although some twirls hung down to decorate her face. Her best features were her large black eyes, which could have hypnotised any man I suspect, and her full red lips, which were moist and succulent and glistened like polished coral.

We did not say much at that time, although I was able to detect, when she thanked me for the application, what I suspected, and later confirmed, was an Italian accent. I noticed at that time a doorway in the back of the shop, which piqued my interest. The door had been removed and replaced with one of those screens of coloured streamers that shops use to obscure any useful view of the contents of the room. The streamers still allowed suggestive glimpses between the gaps, of course. To add to the curiosity a sign above the door frame said: 'Over-18s Only'. I wondered how many under-18s came into the main part of the shop anyway, but said nothing.

I was called in for an interview two days later and this time I was introduced to the same lady for a proper chat. Her name was Valentina and she was most pleasant to me. She led me into her back office and asked me about my previous retail experience. She was very impressed to see that I had done a year in the women's wear department of a large store just after leaving school – she did not seem too concerned that it was over a decade ago. I guessed that applicants with serviceable experience in the field were hard for her to find.

She asked me how I felt about dealing with the odd strange customer and I tried my best to portray an open mind, which I think pleased her to hear. Then I was invited to follow her on a tour of the shop: the stock room was first, followed by the tiny tea-room, then back into the main shop area before the bit I was really curious about: the Over-18s area.

I followed Valentina through the dangling strips into a darker room, with its own counter and cash till. A very gothic-looking girl with black eyeliner looked up and smiled at us as we walked in.

The room was nearly the same size as the main shop, but felt more enclosed with the red paintwork and the fake brickwork design painted over it in black. There were racks and shelves just like in the main shop, but the clothes here were more, well, let me be frank: kinky. There were school uniforms and teachers' gowns of course, but also nurse outfits, serving-wench costumes and all sorts of PVC and leather ensembles with a domineering edge. The shelves were covered with sex toys, videos and magazines, amongst other trinkets.

I was asked if I had a problem with working in this room from time to time, whether that might be embarrassing or uncomfortable for me. I could see why Valentina had felt it prudent to check that candidates were happy with the situation during the interview: just about anyone would be taken aback by being thrown in at this particular deep end on their first day.

Part of the problem with my husband had been boredom. Life in the sack was simply not interesting enough for me, and Patrick was hardly keen to spice things up. I remember I came home with an anklet on once and he told me to take it off because it made me look like a whore. I had only put it on to turn him on, but this was a man who preferred sex to be strictly ready-salted in flavour, and my efforts went unappreciated.

After the divorce came through, I had found some solace in the thought that I was 'out there' again and that having discovered the wrong way that a sex life needs to be interesting, I was determined to spice things up a bit more this time around.

Starting out my new life with a job in what amounted to a sex shop was not what I had had in mind, but, now confronted with it, I felt only curiosity and interest, and yes, even excitement. I told Valentina that I could not wait to start. She seemed very pleased at my answer.

It's obvious from the mere fact that I am relating all of this that I was offered the job, and that, of course, I took it. I worked the week nine to five-thirty in the company of Valentina, and covered at other times if the more casual staff, which she tended to use on Thursday evenings and weekends, were unavailable, ill, or hungover.

The first sex lives to benefit from my new position were those of my friends, whom I encouraged to come into the shop and buy something saucy for their husbands and boyfriends to enjoy. We had a giggly time trying things out and picking just the right garments. It was almost like one of those lingerie parties that some people host in their homes.

Valentina did not mind the lack of decorum while I was selling underwear and hosiery to my friends, indeed I think she welcomed the atmosphere of fun that we brought to the proceedings. Her philosophy, I picked up quite early, was that sex should be light and fun, and that a jovial ambience was more likely to help a bashful customer overcome her reticence and purchase those crotchless knickers they've been dithering about than a quiet, more discreet, secretive atmosphere, which only implies that the customer is doing something they should be ashamed of.

I learned quite a bit about Valentina in my first few weeks. She was originally from Orvieto, and had come to Britain to attend one of our northern universities for her final year. It was one of those courses that took you to a different country each year, and previously she had been studying in Amsterdam, then Berlin, and, finally, Glasgow.

Things had got interesting for her in Amsterdam, when, at a tender nineteen, she had discovered a love of pornography. I think she may have been only the second female I had ever heard admitting to such a preference. Anyway, it began with watching 'party-girl' gangbangs (she would watch and pretend she was the girl getting the seeing-to from three, four, or however many, directions) and then progressed to kinkier and kinkier videos. After lots of experimentation, she discovered that she liked female domination videos the most. Soon she was devouring every S&M source she could lay her hands on until eventually she attended a club. It went disastrously: she felt totally alone and out of place – which surprised me, given her current beauty and confidence – and the idea died for a little while.

On moving to Berlin, however, the urge to try again became too much, so she bit her gorgeous lip and attended a casual S&M meeting in a bar. It went much better, everyone was in plain clothes and the scene was more welcoming, she felt more comfortable and attended their club. Before long she was spending three nights a week dominating German gents and having the time of her life.

On moving to the UK she found clubs and societies here that she still attends now. Her interest in sexuality made it natural that her eventual career would have something to do with everyone's favourite pastime. Opening a lingerie shop with an adult store in the back has nothing to do with the degree she studied for, needless to say.

I tried my best to hide my amazement at her history. You hear rumours about these things going on all around us, but never imagine you might meet someone who's at the centre of it all.

I never asked her what went on at these places; I suppose despite my curiosity I was scared of something, perhaps that I would hear something that would disgust me or even that something taboo would turn me on, I don't know.

Perhaps it was nearly two months into my job before an unexpected hangover amongst the part-time staff meant I was called in to cover on a Saturday. Valentina looked very relieved indeed when I came into the shop at around ten o'clock to rescue her. Herself and a part-timer were trying their best to serve customers on the floor and cover two tills at the same time. It was obvious my presence was going to make a big difference.

I was set to work on the till in the main shop, while Valentina tried to drum up sales by wandering around the shop helping the ladies choose their knockout ensembles. The young part-timer Zoë, who I had never met before, was asked to watch the red room.

Business ticked over healthily for the next few hours and, in addition to the ladies that Valentina and I were serving out in the front, there was a steady trickle of men, and women, heading through the screen for the sex shop. I found myself wondering what sort of items they were carrying away in the plain carrier bags that Zoë had packed everything into.

Then, just after coming back from my lunch, while making the tea, I got quite a shock: a face entering the shop that I recognised. It was Gareth, the husband of one of my best friends, Elaine. Indeed I had brought Elaine into the shop just three weeks before to buy a red and black camisole suspender with matching knickers (we had thrown in a pair of half-price black stockings to go with them) and I wondered at first if Gareth's appearance at the shop was connected to that purchase. I was still in the tea-room behind the counter, and, I don't really know why, instead of going over to say hello, I closed the curtain over and spied on him while the tea brewed.

He was a little furtive, but certainly not the most nervous or uncomfortable male I had seen in the store, and seemed to be browsing the stockings. Valentina came over to offer assistance but he didn't seem too comfortable with the attention and declined. I went back to the tea, adding milks and sugars where appropriate, and took one through to Zoë (through the back entrance) before coming back through to spy on Gareth through the curtain. Valentina would just have to wait for her tea until Gareth had gone away, I decided.

Gareth had now picked up a basket and had a couple or three items in there that he had taken down from the racks. I felt so curious about what they might be I wished I could get a good look at them. He seemed to be finished and began heading for the till, where I hoped against hope Valentina would meet him to ring his items through – that seemed infinitely preferable to the alternative that she might call on me to come out and serve him. My goodness, that would have been an awkward moment.

I was saved though as, at the last minute, he took a turn to the right and slipped through the screen into the adult shop area. I breathed a sigh of relief and emerged, two teas in hand, and passed one to the boss lady. I didn't want to say anything just yet, in case Gareth heard our gossiping through the screen, so instead I took my seat behind the counter and did my best to hide inconspicuously behind my tea.

Gareth was about fifteen minutes in the room; it seemed like an age before he emerged with one of our pink and red carrier bags under his arm, filled with goodies. Leisurely, without a care in the world, he sauntered towards the door, smiling at Valentina on the way. Knowing that I would not have to face him directly was a relief certainly, but I could not just let him leave without making him aware of my presence in some way.

I cooed his name and said hello.

Gareth turned with some surprise to see me waving at him with a playful smirk on my face.

He replied with a mumbled greeting and a nervous smile as he struggled with the door, reddening slightly. I watched him leave the shop, turn left, then change his mind and turn right before slipping away.

Forgive me, but I was curious about what he had bought and, ignoring the questioning eyebrow that Valentina arched in my direction, I slipped into the back room and filled Zoë in on the situation, which, like me, she found quite amusing.

Zoë informed me, to my great surprise, that Gareth was in just about every other Saturday and tended to

153

buy hose from the main shop. Sometimes, but not always, he would purchase a suspender belt too, and then, only occasionally, he would slip into the red-walled room and buy a dildo and lubrication. Today had been just one of those occasions.

On returning to my post, I was given the same information about Gareth by Valentina, who, rather than show any amusement, delivered her view of the customer in more disparaging terms:

'Dirty little perverted sissy-boy,' were her exact words. It was the domina in her I think.

I must admit I was curious about the purpose of Gareth's bag of tricks, but it seemed to me it could just as easily have been intended for use with his wife Elaine and I decided to accept that, ahead of Valentina's interpretation of his behaviour, as the most likely explanation.

I got my chance to find out more three weeks later when I was invited to a party at Elaine's house. There was no occasion really, just one of those dinner parties that people throw now and again to show off their homes or their cooking skills. I mentioned it to Valentina the week before and she insisted on choosing my outfit for me, supplying me with a black dress, seamed black stockings and black lacy underwear from the stock in-store. She even insisted that I bring in a selection of shoes from my wardrobe, to make sure I selected the right pair. She chose a red pair, which surprised me given that I had been told to wear black up to now, and instructed me to wear understated make-up save for prominent red lipstick. I rather suspected she was moulding me into her own image, but she stopped short of telling me to dye my red hair black.

On arriving I ran a marathon of greetings and kisses and, needless to say, curious questions about my ex-husband and my saucy new job, which I tried my best to play down. However, after a couple of drinks, I let it slip that my boss was a dominatrix in her spare time and found myself fielding questions all through dinner. Gareth was suspiciously silent all the while and seemed very uncomfortable indeed with the subject matter, trying his best to start up football or film conversations at his end of the table, but failing miserably.

It was only back in the living room, after dessert, that I got a chance to speak to Gareth directly. I did not really have to seek him out either, he seemed keen to talk to me, whispering that he needed to ask me something. I told him to go ahead of course and, somewhat hesitantly, he went straight in to talk to me about the time I had seen him in the shop. He explained that the items he had bought were to aid the love-making between him and his wife and that Elaine was rather sensitive about it all and would prefer it if I did not mention it.

I must admit I was not altogether convinced; Elaine had not shown any signs of embarrassment in the shop with me a month or so back and I suspected that Gareth had a Secret Love of his own. But I was too tipsy to try and interrogate him for more, indeed it was my tipsiness that was occupying most of my mind at the time. The evening was becoming very couply and I was thinking about leaving soon but I have this thing: I hate being drunk and going home in a taxi – I'm sure I am not alone in this.

I extended a fingernail (bright red of course, as per Valentina's instruction) and ran the tip of it under Gareth's chin and giggled. I told him that the last thing I wanted was to embarrass Elaine and that provided he gave me a lift home, I could not see any problem with his request.

He hesitated at first, seeming rather put out by the insertion of a clause into his request, but he was clearly feeling vulnerable because he agreed without negotiation.

As host, Gareth had not touched any drink so when, an hour later, he announced he was giving me a lift it seemed a logical thing. On the way home I tried my best to subtly question Gareth on the items he had bought in the shop, but I did not want to be too direct and it was a little difficult to find the necessary mental agility to squeeze anything out of him; in his sober state he was one step ahead of me all the way and I completely failed to get anything out of him other than the fact that he and Elaine liked to keep things interesting.

In the end, as we parked outside my home, I just lost my patience and wound up telling him, in something of a drunken outburst, that I knew he was up to something and that I was going to tell Elaine if he wasn't more honest with me.

To my surprise he pleaded with me not to. No begging or anything like that, just an earnest plea not to tell her.

It was at that moment that I first seriously thought Valentina's original suspicions might have foundation. Was Gareth using the items for himself somehow, or worse, for another lover?

I was too drunk to think too hard about it – I just joked that he had better keep me on his good side. I stepped out of the car, thanked him for the lift, joked again about being good to me, wagging my finger and slurring that he should ring me tomorrow for his next assignment, and shut the car door. He waved, I waved, he drove off, I went inside, took something to stave off a hangover, kicked off my red shoes, and went straight to bed in my dress and stockings.

I spent the next day catching up on a late morning. Sundays tend to be my housework days and the extra couple of hours in bed really set me back. I had woken at about ten to the sumptuous sensation of my stockinged legs rubbing together. The strange feeling of the nylon against the cotton of my sheets was something I enjoyed and I became rather regretful that I had not ever tried sleeping in hose before.

Once I had dragged myself from my bed and looked in the mirror, I cursed myself twice, once for not washing my face and once for not removing my tangled and creased dress. I removed my dress and set about cleaning my face in the bathroom, before returning to the bedroom. I was rather reluctant to remove my undergarments, so nice did they feel, and I actually did the dusting in two rooms wearing only knickers, bra, suspender and hose.

I put some proper clothes over them at lunch and continued with the cleaning around the house, stopping for a spot of television or a cup of tea here and there, but before long it was teatime and I still had not touched the bedroom or bathroom.

Rather inconveniently, the phone rang. I debated whether I had time to answer it – it might be my boring ex-husband or perhaps even a relative on for a marathon drone about this, that and the next thing and I could ill afford such an interruption. Heaving a sigh I answered it.

To my surprise, it was Gareth on the line. He whispered hello to me as though worried who might hear on the other end. I asked him what he wanted, and when I got my reply I nearly fell over: he said he was calling me for his assignment.

I nearly laughed to hear my parting joke from the night before being quoted back at me in earnest. But on reflection I am glad I choked it back. Had I laughed at that time perhaps none of what followed would have happened. My initial reply was to ask him to repeat himself, which he did with no little stuttering or nervousness.

My God, I thought, he means it.

The picture started to come into focus: Gareth had a little submissive streak perhaps, spotted so expertly by the boss lady Valentina, and had rather enjoyed me manipulating my taxi ride out of him after the dinner party, so much so that he latched onto my joke like a guard dog to a trouser leg, taking it literally.

The goodies from the shop were clearly nothing to do with Elaine at all, and only for his own private use, to aid whatever fantasy he liked to play out in his mind. I wondered what he did with his sexy underwear and dildo. I could only guess.

Dare I take advantage of him again? Dare I request his presence? Dare I continue this, behind my friend's back? To be frank, I did not consider I was cheating my friend just by blackmailing her husband to do my housework, so I dared. I told him to come straight round.

I had him working right away on the bedroom, changing the sheets, generally tidying the room and wardrobe, putting my shoes into pairs and neatening up my knickers drawer. All the while I sat in the chair in the corner and watched him busying himself while I barked out the odd guiding instruction on how I liked to fold my underwear. As Gareth worked I became more and more curious about what he had been up to with the dildo and the underwear, and decided I was going to get to the bottom of it all.

When he had finished the bedroom I praised him on the job. He asked me if this meant we were quits. I sensed the threat of me telling Elaine about his perversion was foremost in his mind still, and I decided to use it.

I told him that I would promise not to mention anything on the condition that he told me what he used the underwear and dildo for. I dressed the question up in concerns for my friend – that I needed to be certain he wasn't doing anything to hurt her and all that. It was very convincing.

Listening to the reply was like watching an old man get out of an armchair, so difficult did Gareth find it to draw the words out of himself. But I must admire his bravery and, to some extent, his honesty. He told me he liked to be submissive to women and that he got very turned on by playing with their underthings (my eyes bulged at that news and I feared I had made an error of judgement letting him go through my underwear drawer. I glanced at his crotch for signs of a bulge and wondered why I had not noticed it earlier).

It seemed plausible but for one thing: it did not explain the dildo. I quizzed him again on what the dildo was for and he tried to tell me that it really was for Elaine.

I didn't believe him, and I suggested that if that was the case, he wouldn't mind me discussing it with her. He readjusted his answer, admitting with head bowed that he liked to fuck his arse with it while he masturbated. I was shocked that he would tell me this, but I suppose I had asked for it. I noted how aroused he seemed to be while revealing this to me and how the bulge in his trousers twitched. I decided enough was enough: I told him we would speak no more about it, and that he could go.

I would not be human if I had managed to keep this little tale to myself at work on Monday. In between customers I told Valentina every detail I could possibly recall about the weekend and she listened thoughtfully. I noted that not once did she laugh or smile at Gareth's behaviour, rather her tongue rolled around her mouth like a boiled sweet; it was a look of quiet, knowing contemplation.

I finished the story and Valentina just looked at me for a moment as though evaluating me, then she told me flatly that Gareth was a submissive, he liked to wank himself while wearing ladies' underwear and he enjoyed being humiliated by women. There followed a harshly-arched eyebrow as though to admonish me for not concluding this myself.

I suppose that once I had heard it actually being said I realised I had probably known this all along, just never consciously acknowledged it. Valentina pressed the situation, suggesting that I invite him around again, this time with a real dominatrix present and she could show me how I should have dealt with him.

It was very tempting, I must admit, the idea of dominating a man – surely we've all had little urges to control a member of the opposite sex in some way or another. Trouble was, I had some very real worries about the idea: firstly, that Valentina might be wrong in her interpretation, after all, she had only heard things second-hand and, secondly, that I had called it quits with Gareth and I could not see him agreeing to do more housework for me.

Valentina could not have been more disparaging about my fears. She waved a flamboyant Mediterranean hand in front of my face, telling me she could not possibly be wrong and, besides, he would be so eager to serve that it wouldn't matter to him even if I was going back on a deal. I was convinced.

Valentina instructed me to call him and tell him, not ask him, tell him, to come around again as I had some more housework for him to do. I did so, ringing his mobile early that evening, and she was right, he did not hesitate to agree to it. I also told him to bring a bow tie, just as Valentina had suggested I do, and he agreed without hesitation. Now I really believed she was right.

She instructed me to go bare-legged with a pair of black high-heeled courts on and the shortest black skirt I could find: men, she assured me, work harder when they can see an amazing pair of legs out of the corner of their eye. The dark colours contrasting with my white legs would dominate his field of vision, she told me. The top she left to my own choice. I went for a black low-cut affair.

I sent Valentina a text message to let her know when Gareth was due – she had promised to join us half an hour later. In the meantime, I poured myself a glass of white wine and I waited for Gareth to arrive. He was on time and I felt a nervousness shimmer through me as the doorbell chimed. I went to let him in.

'Come in,' I said. He stepped into the hallway.

He looked at me and said hello. I saw him start at the sight of my legs. Again I put Valentina's instructions into action: she had told me to find the neutral gear for my voice, to speak without love or hatred, without heat or cold. This, she said, best gave the impression that I expected, rather than needed or wanted, my instructions to be carried out. I looked him straight in the eye.

'You are to call me Mistress,' I instructed him. 'And after this moment you are not to look me in the eye.'

Gareth closed his eyes and released the sigh of a man whose dreams had come true in one incredible moment. He looked to the floor and voiced his compliance to my new name.

'Follow me,' I said as I strode to the living room. I heard him confirm his compliance and quote my new title again as he followed behind me.

161

I pointed where I wanted him to stand and sitting back in my armchair I placed a graceful hand on my wine glass and crossed my legs torturously slowly.

'Put your bow tie on around your bare neck,' I said as I relaxed into the soft back of the chair.

I watched as his nervous hands pulled his T-shirt collar away from his neck and shakily applied the bow tie just underneath his adam's apple.

'Now remove all of your clothes, except the bow tie,' I decreed.

Gareth was extremely edgy and I watched him down my nose as I sipped my wine. With some difficulty and shakiness he removed all of his clothes. Obediently he stood to attention and just like I had told him he looked straight ahead rather than at me. His penis was half-erect and bouncing slightly with each of his enlivened heartbeats. I love them when they pulsate like that.

'My kitchen needs to be tidied: dishes washed and put away, surfaces bleached and floor mopped. You have half an hour,' I said to him.

He voiced his compliance and respectfully used my title.

My kitchen joins directly onto my living room, so I could watch him make busy while I posed regally in my armchair and savoured my wine. I smiled to myself: I felt fantastic, so powerful, so spoilt, so special, so mean. It was really the first time that I appreciated the joy that had led to Valentina pursuing this lifestyle all those years ago.

Gareth was still doing the floors when I heard Valentina arrive. I was so busy watching his excited, dribbling penis sway like some counter-balancing kangaroo tail as he swept the mop from side to side that I did not hear her car or her footsteps. It was the much louder sound of the doorbell that woke me from my reverie.

Valentina had instructed me on the orders to give our slave at this point; I passed them on: 'Answer the door for me in the following manner: open it wide enough for Mistress Valentina to step inside, then kneel immediately with your eyes downwards. Offer a greeting to the Mistress and wait for her commands,' I said to him.

He scuttled off to the door without hesitation, seemingly relishing the opportunity to perform any task from me. I listened as the door was opened and slave Gareth greeted Mistress Valentina. There was more talking that I did not catch and the door was closed. The next thing I knew, Gareth was crawling back to the centre of the living room where he knelt with his head down. Valentina strutted in behind him in a black pencil skirt to just above the knee, seamed stockings, shoes similar to my own, an emerald-green bodice, a long black coat open at the front, her dark hair scrunched behind her head and a pair of black-rimmed spectacles. She was carrying a carpet bag.

'Good evening, Mistress Susan,' she said, ignoring the slave completely by turning her back to him. 'Has the slave completed his task?'

'Nearly, Mistress,' I said. 'He has just the mopping to finish.'

She turned to Gareth.

'Finish mopping the floor and return to your position,' she said to him. She lit a cigarette and sat in the armchair next to me. I had noticed that her Italian accent was more prevalent than usual. I thought it made her comments sound all the more sexy and I wondered how they sounded to poor Gareth who must have been bubbling with arousal now.

Valentina quietly opened the bag to show me what she had brought with her. I peered inside to see a maid's uniform, some lingerie and hosiery, a riding crop, a pink

163

dildo (of very kind proportions I thought), some leather cuffs and some high-heeled shoes. I had seen all these items on sale in our shop.

Gareth had finished his task and returned to the centre of the floor. I nodded in his direction to let Valentina know.

'Stand. Good. Now remove your bow tie,' she told him. 'Good.'

She stepped over to the naked Gareth, taking the bag with her. She blew smoke on him and deliberately brushed his body as she circled him tantalisingly: her leg brushed his penis and her fingertips ran over his buttocks. I saw his penis winch itself to the horizontal for the first time. Behind him now, Valentina pointed for me to do the same. We spoke about our slave as I repeated her moves, teasing him further.

'I think we have found a good little maid have we not?' she asked.

'Yes, very healthy and capable,' I agreed, brushing his penis with my forearm as I circled him.

'I think he is ready for his uniform, don't you, Mistress Susan?'

'Yes, I do, Mistress Valentina,' I agreed, looking Gareth pointedly in the eye.

Valentina opened the bag and pulled out flesh-coloured stockings, a suspender belt, the uniform and shoes. Together, as though Gareth were some infant girl, we dressed him, rolling the nylons up his legs and fixing the clasps, guiding the heels onto his feet and making him step into the dress, steering his arms through the puffy sleeves and zipping it up. Finally, she made Gareth suck on the dildo to wet it and, lifting the uniform at the back, slipped it inside his anus. The gasp and moan at insertion were the only sounds he made throughout. On Valentina's cue I joined her as we rubbed her hands sensuously on his stockinged legs and told him what a pretty maid he was. His penis was now at full mast and dribbling pre-cum – a tiny spot was seeping through the dress.

'Now I am going to teach Mistress Susan how to treat you, the first of her many slaves,' Valentina announced. 'Get onto the floor like a dog.'

Gareth got down on all fours.

'Mistress Susan's vacuum cleaner is broken, so I need you to pick up all the dust from the carpet with your tongue. Begin.'

Gareth did as he was told, pressing his tongue to the pile, picking up dirt and dust and swallowing it, his arse in the air housing the bright pink dildo.

I felt the riding crop enter my hand and without any hint or suggestion from my teacher I began smacking his buttocks with it to make him go faster. Mistress Valentina laughed and Gareth began to moan with a mix of discomfort and pleasure.

'Beautiful!' laughed Mistress Valentina as I continued the cropping, loving every minute of it.

Gareth was really struggling to keep up with the pace we were demanding of him, and judging from his groans I surmised he had lost control and might come. In response I leant down and began fucking his arse with the dildo. Gareth stopped in his tracks, bending over double with his face in the carpet. I quickened the pace and noticed a sneaky little hand reach between his legs to give his penis a couple of pulls. He came straight away, crying loudly into my carpet.

'Good. Carry on,' instructed Valentina, completely unfazed and unsympathetic to his orgasm recovery.

I began to strike his arse with the crop again and the carpet cleaning recommenced.

'There is a lot of carpet to be cleaned and only one

tongue, so we cannot afford to waste time cleaning semen from slaves' uniforms,' I said.

Valentina nodded and smiled to show her approval. That crop has never left my hand since.

– *Susan, South London, UK*

Going Out With a Bang

I've never been that great at sticking to a job. I get bored easily – and when I get bored I'll do anything to break out of the rut. I get cheeky to managers, and start ignoring the rules. So I end up having to look for a new job. I don't mind; keeps things fresh.

Just don't ever put me on a customer help line. You'd be asking for trouble.

The worst job I ever had wasn't even a proper job; it was an apprenticeship scheme for one of the electricity companies. I don't know how I ended up in that one – probably it was the only thing on the list I hadn't tried before. But it was a big mistake. I thought it was going to be indoor work, but it turned out that the on-the-job training was about going round in a minibus checking on substations to see they hadn't been vandalised and walking under power lines through forests, noting where the trees were growing too close to the cables so some other sod could come cut them down. It was winter, and usually pissing with rain, and always cold. The boys on the course were the only thing that made it worthwhile. I was the only girl out of seven of us, see, and they were a right laugh. Andy, who was in charge of the group, had a hard time keeping us under control sometimes.

I'd decided straight away this was the wrong job for me. I hate the cold, and the stupid reflective clothes they make you wear. I don't want to spend my life bundled up in jumpers and yellow plastic waterproofs with my nose red and running. So I made arrangements behind the scenes to get another job – working in a sandwich shop, as it happens – and I handed in my notice. Then I went out for one last day on the job, so I could say goodbye to the boys.

It was the usual crock as far as the work went – parking up in a muddy lay-by in the middle of nowhere and slogging for miles under dripping trees.

Lee tried to liven it up a bit. He's a joker, he is. 'Watch out, Shell: there's snakes around here.'

'Yeah?'

'They can sneak up and bite you if you're not careful.'

'Right.'

'I reckon there's a few looking at you right now. They go for women, you know.' He grabbed my shoulders suddenly and I jumped. 'Careful!'

His eyes goggled. I sniggered, wriggling out of his grasp. 'What sort of snakes?'

'Trouser snakes!'

We all laughed. But I thought, yeah, being the only girl in a bunch of blokes has its moments. They all pay attention to you. I bet there were a few trouser snakes poking their heads up when I wriggled in and out of my pants on a morning. I always made sure to bend over and give them a look at my bum.

Then we came back to the minibus for our sandwiches at midday. The windows steamed up straight away as we piled into the back of the bus in our damp woollies and regulation plastic anoraks. There were two benches down the sides of the bus and we sat four on one side, three on the other, facing each other. Andy was in the front behind the wheel of course. Daz opened his Thermos of Bovril tea and Mike complained, as usual.

'Smells like you guffed!'

Wedged at the top end of the bus I unzipped my way out of my jacket and leaned forward as I worked it down over my arms. You've got to take some layers off when you're inside, I'd found, or else you just feel colder when you go out again. Rob began to whistle the Stripper music.

'Keep going!' urged Lee, to laughs.

'What?' I looked at them wide-eyed and innocent. Then I pulled up the front of my jumper and the T-shirt underneath to flash them. I felt the cold air slap my skin. I hadn't put a bra on that morning, you see, only our clothes are so bulky no one had noticed. Until then. 'Like this?'

They whooped in shock and there was a lot of appreciative swearing. I've got nice big tits. Andy looked over his shoulder at us and asked sharply: 'What's going on?'

'Nothing!' Mike answered, and the others joined in, insisting we were all totally innocent. I didn't care.

'You think it's too cold for that?' I asked. I pulled my top up again, sticking my tits out so I could look down at them. 'Oh. Yeah. Look, it is cold. They're all hard and pointy.'

'Shell!' hooted Jay. I noticed Ross's jaw was hanging open like he'd been punched; everyone else was grinning. My boobs might be cold but my pussy was hot from the attention I was getting.

'What d'you reckon?' I added, turning to Davo who was sat next to me. Davo's usually pretty quiet; he's quite young with spiked blond hair. 'Want a feel?'

'Ah.' He swallowed. 'Yeah.' He reached out and poked my right nipple with one fingertip, and it was all I could do not to laugh.

'Go on; get a proper feel.'

He put his sandwich box on his knees and groped me properly, with both hands. I wriggled and pushed against him. My nipples were so stiff they ached as he rubbed them. He started grinning so hard it looked like his head was going to fall in half. 'God, yeah!' he muttered.

'Shit, do we all get a go?' Lee asked.

'Don't see why not.' I pulled my jumper right off over my head, letting my breasts bounce free. It was cold in that minibus but it was worth it for the looks on their faces as I cupped my tits and jiggled them together.

'Michelle!' squealed Andy. He was trying to sound disapproving I guess.

'What?' I snapped testily.

'What do you think you're doing?'

'Having a bit of fun.'

'Put that lot back on!'

I turned to face him. He was hunched over the back of his seat, red-faced. 'What's your problem? I handed in my notice, didn't I? What you going to do – sack me?'

He gaped, his eyes fixed on my big bare tits. I backed off down the centre aisle until I was in the middle of the bus. There wasn't much room between the two rows of knees.

'Who wants some then?' I asked, keeping a defiant eye on Andy but sinking to my own knees on the floor so they could all reach. 'Go on, guys; get a handful of my tits.'

They did. I forgot to watch our supervisor. They reached in from both sides to play with my bubbies, rolling and bouncing and tugging them. Mike's hands were icy but gentle, Jay's hard and rough, Daz liked to twist my nipples like they were radio dials. They took liberties too, groping down my belly and back to the elastic waist of my trousers. 'I love being touched,' I gasped over their noises of pleasure. 'Go on, touch my titties.'

'Jesus,' said Davo miserably. 'I've got a woody.'

My eyes flashed open. 'Want me to do something about that?' I was betting he wasn't the only one with that problem.

'What?' He stared round the other guys. 'Like, here?'

'Get it out so I can have a look, Davo.'

There were sniggers, and calls of encouragement. Davo looked at Andy, but our boss had turned away and was staring out the front windscreen – the back of his neck was the colour of brick. Davo groped at the bulging front of his pants. I walked forward on my knees to help him, and he let me pull his waterproofs down and unbutton his fly. Out popped a slim rosy-coloured cock with a sticky eye that winked at me.

'I got a girlfriend,' Davo muttered.

'Don't worry. I'll just suck it. Doesn't count.' He smiled, not sure if I was joking. I took hold of his cock, knowing that his spunk was boiling in his nuts, and glanced round at the others. 'When I've finished with Davo I want to see the rest of you ready for me.'

'Christ, Shell . . . You mean it?'

'Shut up – you heard her!' said Davo.

I was pleased they all went for their trousers at that. I was itching for the eager hard cocks that were brought out into the light. I wanted to taste their come. Six blokes. Would they all taste different? I licked my lips, promising I'd get back to them soon.

'And will somebody get my bloody pants down for me?'

I turned back to Davo and while I was busy getting my mouth round his dick other hands pulled my waterproofs down to my knees, reached under to pop my fly-button, yanked down my jeans and my knickers.

I felt icy air on my wet slash. I squealed around Davo's cock when they touched me on the asshole and in the juicy split below it. Fingers were all over me, rudely spreading my bum-cheeks and taking liberties in the place the sun don't shine. I reckon it was pretty impressive that I kept enough concentration on the hot cock in my mouth, what with fingers sliding into me and making me wetter and wetter. There was a lot of muttering and laughing and encouraging noises going on over my head, but I couldn't really pay it attention because Davo was rigid as a board under my pumping head. But I heard Lee's voice.

'Cover me, men: I'm going in.'

Always the joker, Lee. He was on the opposite bench. He picked me up by the hips and without pulling my mouth off Davo's cock planted my backside in his lap and pushed his own dick right up my wet hole. I was a bit surprised how big he was, to be honest. I made this groaning noise and Davo came in my mouth right at that moment, hot and salty and squirting right up the back of my nose because I got my breathing all wrong in my surprise.

I had to hang on to Davo's hips while Lee fucked me from behind. I had more respect for his trouser snake after that.

They all got their go. I sat on Ross's lap, facing out, and bounced up and down so they could all watch my tits slamming back and forth as he pumped into me. I knelt on the floor, feeling the ridged metal all gritty and wet under my knees as I gave Mike a blow job and Daz spanked my splayed ass with his hand. Daz was into butts; he got entry to my bum-hole, though once he was up there he came so fast I reckon he'd never had the chance before. Jay's was the best from my point of view though: he got the others to sit on the edge of the benches and hold me on their knees while I lay stretched out, my head tipped back. Jay's big and muscley and has a shaven head and tattoos; definitely the best body out of the lot of them. He knelt over me and fucked me down the throat while the others played with my tits and cunt, and held me down when I started squealing and thrashing. I liked that. It felt like they were all fucking me at once.

Some of them even came back for second goes. I can just imagine what it would have looked like to passing drivers; the minibus at the side of the road with the steamed-up windows, rocking from side to side as they fucked me in turn, or together.

And Andy? Andy couldn't approve of this at all. Andy was above that sort of thing. He sat behind the wheel with the rear-view mirror tilted to he could see everything going on behind him, and jacked off on his own.

We didn't get any more work done that afternoon of course. We drove back to town good and tired though – and I was sticky all over with come, and my lips were swollen and I felt like I wouldn't walk straight for a week. Six young men had fucked me good and hard. Now that's what I call a proper job. They gave me a huge cheer as they dropped me off at my bus-stop, and wolf-whistled out the windows all the way down the road till the bus was out of sight.

I might not be very good at keeping down a job, but people are always sorry to see me go.

– *Michelle, Bath, UK*

Hair My Song

I was standing on the rocky outcropping, taking in the breathtaking view of the pristine forest valley below, when my nose suddenly started twitching with something more than just pine scent. I looked to the right, the left, behind at an approximate south-southeast angle.

And saw *her* standing there under the hot sun. A hot blonde in hiking shorts and tank top, tangling with a handful of tent poles, her long sun-browned legs and arms stretching out as far as the bedazzled eye could see. She was about two hundred feet away from me, having one hell of a time setting up her tent – a damsel in distress waiting to be rescued by a knight in shiny denim (an experienced hiker, camper, and all-round nature, and woman, lover).

I made tracks for her, off the heated rock shelf and down a path of pine needles that skirted the tall trees. And as I drew nearer, I caught more of the scent of her perfumed perspiration in the downwind draft, saw more clearly how the nipple-poked front of her top and cheek-cleaved back of her shorts were soaked with sweat. And I heard plenty of her exasperated female grunts and groans as she struggled mightily to set up camp.

Then my fine-tuned senses overloaded because, as I crept closer, I got a glimpse of something even more spectacular than the scenery, something that sent me reeling against a tree as my legs gave way: the hair on her arms – and legs.

I clung to the birch bark, maybe twenty feet away now from the tall lean blonde spotlighted in the glowing rays of Old Sol. Staring at her, at the downy straw-coloured hair on her lithe arms and legs that stood up and trembled in the warm breeze, stood out highlighted by the slanting sun; the golden fleece on her limbs that signified that here was a woman who didn't shave. An all-natural woman. My kind of woman.

I hugged the tree trunk in a head-swimming fever, gasping, panting, as the blonde babe lifted a tent pole over her head in an effort to straighten it – and revealed the blonde hair of her armpits. A sight as beautiful as any in nature to the hair-mad man in constant pursuit of the hirsute woman.

Now, to the average person – the men who insist their women be shorn of most, if not all, of their body hair; and the women who do the brutal unnatural shaving in the interests of fashion and social acceptance – I'm a pervert, my fetish for hairy women deemed to be something decidedly dirty, if not downright disgusting.

But call me a caveman if you will. To each his own, I say, and to me go the glories of the soft scented springy fur of the unshaven female leg and arm, and underarm, and pussy. Nothing turns me on more than a woman with a fine dusting of hair on her limbs, a thicker thatch in her armpits, a dense jungle in between her legs. And nothing turns me off more than a woman razor-burned raw of all her natural matting, shaved to some sort of sterile pre-pubescent ideal that looks as cold as it leaves me.

175

The soft-whorl feel of a woman's hair-natural legs and arms; the sweaty tongue-tickling nostril-flaring taste and smell of her hairy underarms; the nose-burying mouth-filling dewy musky delight of a woman's fully-bloomed bush. These are the things I'm forever in search of. A search that has sent me all over Old Europe and new North Africa, seen me purchase more vintage porn than my credit card cares to think of, to satisfy my hair-trigger sexual desires.

And here I'd found a furred female almost right in my own backyard. I shook with excitement.

I didn't know if maybe the babe had just been too long in the bush, or if this was her natural hairified state. But I was bound and determined to find out. So I pushed off from my wooden crutch and cried, 'N-need any h-help?'

She turned and looked at me, startled. Then flashed a dazzling smile. 'Help? Yes, please!'

Her name was Bonita, and she was new to the country. And the backcountry. But she'd wanted to get away from her stuffy apartment in the gritty city for the weekend and out into the great open outdoors.

I applauded her enterprise, standing right next to her, eyes fixed and staring, mouth drooling, openly admiring her lean bronzed blonde-trimmed arms and legs.

'You . . . were going to help me put up tent?' she said, when I'd been glaring at her wonderfully hirsute limbs for a solid sunbaked minute or more.

'Huh? Oh, yeah, sure,' I mumbled, tearing my orbs off her body Velcro and looking up into her wide sky-blue eyes.

I took charge of the poles and nylon and proceeded to speed-rig the two-person sleep-shelter in about two minutes flat. I still have my Boy Scouts camping badge at home, with all the rest.

'Wow! That was quick!' Bonita enthused. She hugged me, mouthing sweet thank yous into my burning ear.

I clutched at her arms as she broke away from me, my fingers trailing over her hair-sprinkled skin from forearms to backs of the hands. 'No problem,' I breathed, holding onto her hands and swinging her arms, ecstatic at the way the wind rustled her down, the way the sun glinted off the pale curly-cues.

She suddenly yawned, kittenish and kitten-pink. 'Sorry!' she blurted, pulling her hands away and covering up her mouth. 'I've been hiking all day. Very worn out.'

And unable to resist, she reached up and arched her back, really stretched. Putting those moist, matted armpits on display for my erotic viewing pleasure.

My knees went to jelly in my jeans, cock swelling. I stared. And stared. Until I caught Bonita's shining blue eyes peeking out from around her outstretched arms.

'You like . . . unshaven, don't you?'

I swallowed, hard; nodded, harder.

She grinned, arms still raised, beads of perspiration trickling down through her hairy underarms, down her sides and into her soaked top. 'You can touch, if you want.'

My mouth dropped open in a silent roar of exultation. I extended my shaking hands and touched her upraised elbows, ran my trembling fingers down the smooth, slick skin of her upper arm and into the glorious tangle of her armpits. We gasped together.

Her arms shook overhead, as I sifted my twitching fingertips through the damp darker-blonde longer hair of her underarms, exploring one of the most hidden vulnerable sexual soft spots on a woman with my sensitive fingers. My cock was now fully tenting my jeans, no assembly required.

177

Bonita was breathing as hard as I was. Then she almost choked when I pushed my head forward and planted my face in her right armpit. I joyously burrowed my nose into the clingy hair of her underarm, inhaling deep of the tangy scent, savoring the ticklish feel. Then I stuck out my tongue and licked at the woman's pale underskin, swirling all through the tangled hair of her one armpit. Then the other.

Bonita moaned, her entire slender body trembling like her slender arms now, as I painted her fur-lined pits with my dragging tongue, licking up from where the hair started to where the hair ended in bold eager strokes. Consuming her salty-sweet perspiration, nipping at the bunched strands of feminine fur.

I only let up when Bonita let her arms tumble down, unable to take the heavy tongue-petting any longer. I quickly dropped to my knees and grabbed onto her bristling legs, started stroking. Running my hands up and down the hairy satiny skin, thrilling at the wispy feel of the sun-blanched short n' curlies.

'You're beautiful! Beautiful!' I groaned, digging my dirty fingernails into Bonita's lean-muscled thighs and urgently lapping at her coat of lighter blonde.

'Oh ... my!' she moaned back, grabbing onto my bobbing head to steady herself.

I sank my teeth into the taut fuzzed flesh of a thigh. Then let the skin fall out of my mouth, hair tickling my teeth and tongue, the roof of my mouth. I kissed and licked and bit into her other hairy thigh, swirling up tufts of blonde with my tongue and tugging on them with my mouth.

Then I gripped the woman's vibrating legs around the bare clenched calves and licked long and hard up her towering follicled lower limbs. From skinny shin to meaty thigh-high. Over and over. Only stopping when

178

Bonita collapsed down to my level on the forest floor, unable to stand any more.

She stared at me from her knees, her eyes wide and inquiring, our sweaty faces inches apart.

I could've kissed her, I guess. But she *didn't* have a mustache.

So, instead, I said, '69?' Using the international language of erotic numbers.

She hit the ground flat, and I straddled her head, grabbing onto her fuzzy thighs again. She yanked my zipper open and dug around in my jockeys, coming up with my hardwood and pulling it down to her lips. I surged with heat as she took my cap into the wet-hot cauldron of her mouth, followed by my shaft.

And as she vigorously sucked on my pulsating dong, I whisked her shorts down, exposing the deliciously dank overgrown garden between her legs that I'd scented from the first. I stared at the rank jungle of blonde pubes, tingling all over with the hairy sight, the musky smell of that matted thatch, the wet pull of Bonita's lips on my prick. Then I dropped my head down and dove tongue-first into her furry snatch.

She moaned from around my cock when I speared through her bush and into her juicy slit, her voice throbbing all through me. Then she groaned when I scooped up the slickened meat of her pussy lips and as much fur as I could handle in the suction of my mouth and indulged in that pinnacle of sexual taste – the hair-pie.

I sucked on her lips, her clit, licked at her slit, tugged on her fur, burying my burning face in that humid blonde forest of pubic hair and breathing deep of the rich raunchy scent, savoring the sticky sweetness of her pussy juices, reveling in the whole delectably furry mess, as she dug her fingers into my jeaned ass and wet-vacced

179

my pulsing cock, her head bouncing off the ground with every deep downward mouth-stroke.

'Fuck!' I grunted into the steaming mash, voice muffled by clotted fur. 'I'm gonna come!'

The heady taste, smell, and feel of Bonita's dripping all-natural pussy, her urgent pulling on my prick, was just too much to resist for too long.

But she beat me to it, her lithe body jumping beneath my tongue, up against my chin, hot spicy juices spilling out of her fur-lined slit and into my gulping mouth.

She whimpered her joy, but didn't let up for a moment on her ferocious blow job, taking me whole to the tightened sack and back down to the bloated cap, over and over, wet-stroking my boiling shaft with her lips and tongue until I howled ecstasy into her swamp pussy, blasting sperm into her milking mouth in heavy heated gouts.

Afterwards, we lay in each other's arms inside the tent. Bonita stroked my bald head, caressed my hairless body, perceptively suggesting to me in her broken-English that maybe my utter denudity had something to do with my raging body hair fetish. I just tenderly petted her furry arms and legs, rubbed her curly pussy, not really listening.

– Darren, Virginia, USA

180

Neighbourhood Watch

It all started by accident. At least, that's what I thought at the time.

I'd just moved into a new house – my very first house! – and was unpacking some boxes in the upstairs bedroom where I planned to sleep. It was night, late, but not too late, when I heard the unmistakable gasps, groans and spring creakings that could mean only one of two things: either my next-door neighbours were redecorating their bedroom, or they were having sex.

Sex it was.

I confirmed that fact quite clearly when I parted a couple of closed blinds on the Venetian window dressing and peeked through the gap. Right through the lacy half-open curtains of the neighbour's half-open window and into their brightly-lit bedroom.

A naked woman was on top of a naked man on top of a comfort-clothed bed, the woman riding the laid-out guy like a crazed cowgirl, her large breasts and long red hair flying, the man gripping her waist and churning his hips, his cock in her pussy, the bed bouncing and groaning like the both of them.

I was only about ten feet removed from the sizzling sex scene, and on the same level. All of the houses on the 'old stock' block were built close together. And what

I'd thought was going to be a problem when I'd first looked over the house was turning out to be anything but.

My prying fingers shook, rattling the blinds. Should I stay or should I go? Was this any way to meet my new neighbours, get to know them? 'Hi, I saw you two having crazy sex in your bedroom last night. I'm Trina, your new next-door neighbour.'

I glanced back at all those boring unpacked boxes. Then looked ahead again, at that candid scorching bedroom romp. My pussy dampened, my whole body heating up nice and tingly, making my decision an easy one.

I resumed spying on my neighbours full-bore, knowing that I'd never get any work done with all that noise going on over there, anyway.

The man on his back with his hands and prick full of joyous redhead appeared to be in his late-twenties. He had shoulder-length brown hair, a lean toned body, and the cock surging back and forth in his partner's pussy was long and hard and thick, gloriously slick with the woman's juices.

She was about his age, but built along plumper, more voluptuous lines, full-bodied and breasted. She was gripping her bounding boobs as she rode the man's saddlehorn, twisting and pulling on her nipples, big butt shuddering and big mouth shouting a chorus of dirty talk that would've drowned out a choir of alley cats.

I was wearing just a ragged old tee and cut-off jeans; appropriate for lugging around boxes and furniture, but obviously overdressed for the present occasion. So, as I stared at my lusty neighbours through the slit in the blinds, I rolled up my T-shirt, opened and lowered my shorts, then really put my right hand to work, sliding it up and under a bare breast, cupping and squeezing.

182

I gasped, the sensation electric. I'd never realized just how exciting voyeurism could be, not being a practitioner up to that point. My legs trembled and my exposed pussy suffused with warm wonderful wetness as I kneaded my tingling breasts, fingered up to a nipple and pinched, rolled. 'Yeeesss!' I exhaled, the pink bud a buzzing length of hardened rubber.

Red let out a whoop of her own from across the way, and sort of slumped over her man, digging her red-painted nails into the grunting guy's smooth muscle-humped chest and halting her bucking. He kept right on fucking though. Actually, picked up the pace, grasping her butt cheeks and pistoning his cock, setting her bum and body to shivering with every hard quick thrust.

I urgently groped my chest, mauling my brimming B-cuppers, pulling on my electrified nipples before taking the final plunge into good neighbour territory – diving my hand down off my heaving chest and onto my smoldering pussy.

'Mmmm-hmmm!' I murmured, fingers bumping button and bursting me full of pleasure.

I was as wet as that cock-rodeoing cowgirl next door, my clit already swollen to orgasmic proportions. I stroked myself fast and hard, like the brown-haired stud filling the need of his filly ten feet away.

The whole window covering started dancing to the tune of my jumping fingers and body as I buffed my button, sweat streaming off my forehead and into my staring eyes. Red was all over the man now, her big tits pressing into his hunky chest. She clutched at his hair, sucked on his tongue as he absolutely pounded her pussy, cock-stroking at full speed, his balls flying and knuckles blazing white on her ass.

I frantically rubbed myself, desperate to keep up, yet desperate to maintain my voyeuristic vigil for as long as possible.

I quickly rubbed myself out, wailing, 'Ohmigod, yes!' my clit exploding under the pressure.

I shook like I was plugged into the wall socket just below my wet white-hot orgasm tidal-waving through my burning body just as Red threw back her head and howled, the brown-haired man grunting and jerking beneath her – the sexy couple delivering a fitting climax to their eye-popping peepshow.

Their names were Clyde and Rachel, husband and wife. I exchanged introductory pleasantries with them on my hurried way to work the next morning. Then hunkered down to some hopeful voyeurism that evening after work.

I set up a comfortable chair and a small folding table in front of the blinds, placing my favourite beverage and vibrator on top of the table, myself in the chair.

Naughty neighbourhood watch by a closet pervert? Perhaps.

All I knew was that I wanted me some more of what I'd seen, and felt, last night – an adult late show that left nothing to the imagination. It was my house and my window, after all.

And it was a full hour of idle sipping and toying before the curtain finally rose on the action next door. Actually, when I pressed the 'glow' button on my watch, I saw that it was the exact same time as the previous evening. Showtime!

Rachel ran through the open bedroom door with Clyde in hot pursuit, both of them laughing. Then kissing, then frenching. Rachel was attired for tonight's performance in a green form-fitting dress, her curvy body almost busting the seams, while my guy Clyde was clad in a pair of faded skin-tight jeans and a bright white tee which splendidly showed off his muscles and tan, and bulge.

He was pressing that bulge into Rachel's stomach, rubbing those bursting seams on Rachel's dress with his big strong hands, as they happily swirled their tongues together. He grabbed onto Rachel's bubbled butt cheeks and lifted her clear off the floor and into his hungry mouth. Rachel moaned, running her fingers through Clyde's glossy hair, her emerald-embossed nails up and down his back.

Heated preliminaries over, they proceeded to tear each other's clothes off, getting naked as the night before in the time it took me to adjust my slimline vibrator to maximum pleasure mode. I was already ahead of the game, though, completely and utterly nude to begin with.

I carefully calibrated the blinds with the hanging stick, so that I had a clear, almost concealed view. My oversexed neighbours had their curtains and window open again, their bedroom lit up like a porn shoot. I leaned back in my swivel chair and spread my legs, slid the humming purple pussy-pleaser down to my glistening pink lips.

I jumped, moaned, as I played the vibrating plastic over my pussy, working my breasts with my other hand, their pointed tips with my fingers. Rachel was down on her knees now on the Oriental throw rug, Clyde's magnificent erection in her stroking hand.

'Suck it! Suck his big hard cock!' I hissed from ten feet and two widened eyes away. I pushed my own pre-formed hard-on into my soaking pussy, slow and sensual and oh-so-filling.

Rachel took Clyde's mushroomed hood into her mouth, tugged on it with her thick lips. Clyde groaned, grasping at his wife's fiery locks.

I pumped, sure and steady, fondling my boobs and nips, heavy and sweaty. As Rachel inhaled her husband's entire swollen length in one heady headlong rush, I gasped, pumping harder, envying the lucky woman who'd obviously had so much practice with the real thing.

She pulled her head back, letting Clyde's meat glide out of her mouth like a glistening snake glides out of its den. His cock dangled there in front of her, huge and slick, until the agonized man jerked Rachel's head closer, and she took him into her mouth again, began sucking in earnest. She gripped his clenched butt cheeks and drove her head back and forth, Clyde shaking in the wet heated grasp of her hands and mouth.

'Yeah, suck his cock! Blow him 'til he blows hot come in your mouth, slut!' I urged, none-too-quietly, pinching a nipple so hard it almost popped off, slamming my pussy.

Then I froze like a dirty deer caught in the headlights of someone's private property.

Because Rachel and Clyde had both turned their heads my way, were looking directly at me behind the slitted blinds, Clyde's cock pointing accusingly. My cover had been blown.

I held my breath, vibrator half-buried in my pussy, hand full of tit.

And the two spied-on lovers ... beckoned at me, simultaneously crooking their fingers in clear invitation. They knew what I was up to, and they wanted me more closely involved in the action!

I hesitated, gazing at their smiling faces, the hanging, shining exclamation point on Clyde's studly body. Then I bolted, throwing a robe over my recharged bod and streaking down the stairs and over to my neighbours.

They welcomed me with open arms, admitting that they'd seen me lurking behind the blinds the night before, as well. In fact, their open curtains and bright bedroom lighting was all in an effort to attract this horny bee to their honey.

I complimented them on their ingenuity, ogling the chiseled Clyde from up-close, my pussy squirming for all that real-man erection. But then my heart and heat level sunk when my new best neighbours requested that I stand back and watch, not touch.

They positioned me next to their bed while they climbed aboard. Clyde quickly plunged his cock into Rachel's pussy from behind, the two doing it doggy-style right in front of me.

I swallowed my disappointment (figuring that we'd be easing into the threesome thing at some later date), and watched and rubbed again. Three feet away from where Clyde was vigorously banging his wife from behind, I sank two fingers into my juiced-up slit and pumped like he was pumping, thumbing my clit, clutching my breasts.

He grinned at me, gripping Rachel's fleshy waist and really flinging himself into the erotic job, his cock flashing in and out of her sucking, ginger-furred pussy. Her butt cheeks rippled in rhythm to his smacking thighs, her face buried in the pillows, a hand in between her legs, rubbing her clit.

The sex-funked room swum before my bleary eyes, the furnace heat from the fucking couple so close sending me scaling new heights of delight with my flying fingers and thumb. I moaned, low and long, a wet hot wave of ecstasy welling up from my overbuffed button and crashing through my quivering body. Coming right alongside my naughty neighbours.

I never have participated. They won't let me. Apparently, they get off on having someone watch their frenzied coupling – as closely as possible – but they don't want to risk their relationship by having that third person actually become involved in the sexing.

I can respect that. Because ever since I moved in next to the pair, I've experienced more passion than I'd ever thought possible – from them and me.

– Trina, Vancouver, Canada

After the Party

I'm a student nurse, and we're supposed to know how to party hard, but this wasn't a nurses' party, it was my best friend's from back at school. So I'd travelled down on the train to her new place in Birmingham. I was between boyfriends at the time and on my own, but there were plenty of people I remembered back from school, even if they had changed a bit now they had real jobs, as well as loads of people from Kay's new office that I didn't know. Probably too many people for a narrow terraced house, to be honest, but we all squeezed in somehow. There was an overflow of smokers in the garden even though it was a cool night. Kay didn't let them do it in the house.

Anyway, I was having a good time. There were plenty of blokes who were happy to get me drink and chat to me, because I was wearing my shortest dress, a little turquoise shift that showed off my bare legs. I'm sort of naturally short and slim, with little hands and slender legs (though I'm stronger than I look: I have to be, to be a nurse) and I bet a whole lot of them were picturing me still in school uniform. I enjoyed finding out what people had done over the last few years and talking about what we remembered of school. Kay had burnt a load of CDs with music we remembered from end-of-term discos.

The men weren't the only ones giving me the eye. There was this woman that I didn't know, a bit older than the rest of us but very pretty, with big lush lips, who gave me the once-over as we moved round each other in the kitchen, and she definitely looked down my top as I knelt to find a glass in the bottom cupboard.

'Love the dress.'

Then she smiled and took the arm of the bloke she was with and steered him away.

'Who's she?' I asked Kay later when we were back in the living room. 'The one with all the lipstick?' She'd kept looking over at me, and I wasn't sure why. It wasn't as if I was flirting with her boyfriend, because he was OK, just nothing special.

'That's Lena, my line manager.'

'You asked your manager to your birthday party?'

'She's OK. She's fun, like.'

Kay was distracted by someone shouting that the pizzas had arrived. I went back to partying. I didn't see Lena again, until much later when I went upstairs to the top-floor toilet to avoid the queue at the ground-floor one. She and her boyfriend were up there in a shadowy corner of the corridor. He was sitting on a blanket-box and she was kneeling astride his lap, face to face with him, their tongues intertwined in a long kiss. I don't know if there was anything really going on there – I didn't stand and watch or anything – but he'd pulled her skirt up at the back to get his hand on her bare cheek and it wasn't like I could miss an eyeful of her knickers and her bum. Big brown bum, snowy white panty-gusset.

She pulled away from the kiss and looked at me.

''Scuse me,' I mumbled, hurrying past, self-conscious despite the buzz of alcohol.

She gave me a slow grin. Now I've never done anything with another girl, never even thought about it really, but that wicked smile made me flush all hot. I hid in the bathroom but it was a while before I could relax enough to pee.

When I came out again the corridor was empty except for two girls waiting to use the toilet.

I didn't last long that night. I'd pulled a horrible series of shifts that week and I was more exhausted than drunk when I decided to call it a night. Most guests were going home but others were staying for the long haul and crashing wherever there was room. Because I gave in quite early I got the pick of the mattresses, so I ended up kicking off my shoes and crawling under the duvet in the spare bedroom. It was a double bed but I didn't take up much of it.

I woke up when someone got into the bed beside me. It didn't occur to me to be worried, just irritated at having been disturbed.

'It's all right; she's asleep!' That was in a loud whisper, followed by a giggle.

So there were two of them. Lying on my back, I kept my eyes shut and waited for them to settle down so I could drift off again. No chance of that happening, though. It quickly became obvious that they hadn't come to bed to sleep. I could smell beer and perfume and a male body. I could hear wet kisses and breathy little mutters of appreciation.

Bloody hell. They were going to fuck right next to me. I had to hold back a snort. I mean it was funny, I guess, but it was a bit awkward for me. What was I supposed to do – just pretend politely to be asleep?

'C'mon.'

'Yeah?'

'Let's do it.'

There was shuffling, the mattress heaved, I heard a soft slap and the clink of a belt being undone. The duvet was pulled right off me. If they thought they were being subtle they must be *really* drunk. Murmurs of 'Oh yes,' and 'That's good, baby,' made me clench my teeth. I was exasperated but curious, itching to see what was going on.

In the end I just opened my eyes. I didn't say anything or make a fuss. I figured they weren't the shy type. In fact they didn't even see me looking, because they were too busy. He was lying on his back alongside me. And Lena – I hadn't recognised her voice, but it was her there in the dim light – was crouched low over him, eyes rapturously closed, sucking his cock.

He had a big meaty cock. Even in that light I could see it glisten with her saliva as she slid those pouty lips up and down his shaft. He rumbled with pleasure deep in his chest. She parted her lips to reveal the fat helmet and swirled her tongue lovingly around it like she was lapping ice cream. Then she dived, taking his length right down her throat as her nose brushed his thick pubic hair.

I was holding my breath just as she must be. I could feel the stir of hot interest in my own body. My arm could have stretched out and touched his where he lay next to me. This was horny as hell, watching her give him head so close by, unaware that I was watching. I wondered what he tasted like between those glossy lips. I wondered how hot his cock was. I wondered what it felt like to have Lena's mouth sucking and kissing and slurping as it did.

But she got bored of being the one doing all the work. Pulling her mouth away, she pumped him in her hand a couple of times. His prick lolled about, thick but not particularly stiff it seemed to me. Then she rose up and straddled him, lifting her skirt up her round thighs to slide his cock into her pussy. I could actually hear the wet noise it made as she positioned it. She must have been ready for him.

Sitting up, it was obvious that he'd been playing with her tits. Her blouse was unbuttoned, her big tits already pulled free of their bra cups to bounce as she rode him, her nipples poking out fat and juicy. She shook back her hair and grabbed his hand to place it on her muff as she rose and fell on him. His hand stirred lazily, then fell away. She twisted her hips, trying to work him in deeper.

Then I heard it.

He *snored*.

Lena stopped gyrating and glared down at her man. I could see the frustration on her face. She slapped his ribs, loudly, and pinched him.

He snored again, on a deeper note.

'Bastard!' she whispered, agonised.

Then she noticed me watching. Her dark eyes were completely black in the dim light. She leaned forward on her fists, bending over me. I could smell the spice of her pussy juices. I didn't know what to say so I just lay there.

She put her hand lightly on my thigh, and stroked my sex-lips through my clothes. I shivered. My nipples, exposed to the cool night after the warm duvet, had tightened to little points that ached at her touch when she caressed me up and down.

Lena clearly decided that if she couldn't have one thing she'd have the other. Sliding off her boyfriend's plump but drooping cock, she wriggled down into the space between him and me. She lifted my skirt, smiling, and kissed my cheek as she slid her fingers over my knickers and down into the warm velvety space between my thighs. I whimpered a little, shocked by myself as much as by her. But I couldn't resist her. She stroked my pussy until I was wet and open, and then she teased my slippery hole and clit until I parted my thighs to invite her deeper. Lying on her side, her back braced against her boyfriend's body, she made me ooze with pleasure until my knicker gusset was soaked.

Then she guided my hand to her. I'd never done this before. I'd never touched a girl except at work, with latex gloves on. I was scared by how hot and wet and raw she felt, how big and ripe was her clit. I was shocked by how much of a hole her bloke had bored into her.

She pushed my fingers inside her.

'C'mon,' she whispered. 'Push. All of them.'

My eyes widened.

'Fill me up,' she urged. 'I can take it, girl. You've got tiny little hands.'

Bunching my fingertips together I pressed into her. I was nervous as hell, but she took my wrist and didn't let me back out. I felt her pussy stretching to take my fingers, tight and hot and muscular as a mouth. Somehow she took them all – right over my knuckles and thumb, the broadest part of my hand. I sank into her up to my wrist.

'Oh yes!' She churned her hips. The sensation was amazing; she was wet and incredibly tight, the muscles of her sex clamping down so hard around my wrist that it felt like I was being crushed, the hot vacuum inside her sucking so hard I thought I might never get my hand back. She groaned with pleasure, pumping me inside her, rubbing her clit with her free hand. But she never forgot to keep touching me. We worked each other, face to face, our breasts bumping through my sweat-soaked dress, her soft lips on my face, until we both came, noisily. And all the time her boyfriend snored drunkenly on. He didn't know what he was missing.

– *Shelley, Wirral, UK*

The Cage

The one sex toy I had always wanted was a custom-built cage. But that kind of metalwork is pricey. I had never been in a position to afford one until one year I got an unexpected tax rebate. Suddenly I had some spare cash and nothing in particular I needed to spend it on. And that cage was finally within reach.

I shopped around and, in the end, probably ended up taking three months before placing my order. And then all I could do was wait. Wait and wait another six whole weeks while a mysterious far-away metal worker did his magic.

But then, it was perfect. It arrived one afternoon, unannounced in an unmarked van and the delivery driver was good enough to bring it down the steps to my basement flat without making a single remark about what on earth I might want it for.

I had him put it in my bedroom.

It was a beautiful cage. Just as I had specified and just as I had imagined over and over before that.

It was steel. Shining silver steel. Rigid bars. A door that clanged nicely and shut firmly with two padlocks securing it. Anyone who had the misfortune to find themselves trapped inside would have no possible means of escape.

The cage also had – and this was my own specifica-
tion – a small hatch in each side and the top, each one
about one foot square. The hatches were designed so
that – if I chose – I could toy with my prisoners any way
I wanted. I think of everything.

The cage sat there in my bedroom, empty, for about
a week. I got turned on just looking at it, imagining. It
took me about that long to decide exactly what I wanted
to do with it now it was mine. I'd always known I
wanted a man in that cage, of course, but what sort of
man? And for how long?

My final decision was that he needed to be beautiful.
He just needed to be beautiful in exactly the right way
and able to spare me maybe one weekend a month. I
had no desire for someone permanently in that cage. Or
in my life. No. Just the odd, intense, brief little episode.
At least, that was what I wanted for now.

And with a little help from the internet and a few select
kinky websites, I found him. His name was Gem. He
was youthful and good-looking. He had submissive and
masochistic fantasies that he wanted to explore, but was
also too busy to devote himself to a full-time relationship. In his emails, the way he expressed himself was
perfect. And when I met him, in a local pub, I knew he
was the one.

He was sweet-looking. Just like the picture he'd sent
me. His pouty lips and shaggy hair made him look
younger than his twenty-seven years. He had a slim little
body, which I later found out was set off with creamy
smooth skin and a little dark body hair, finished with
the cutest tightest little arse. An arse that just begged for
more attention from me, and the kind of attention I
loved to give a guy with a cute arse, but that would
come later. Right now I just wanted him for the cage.

After some preliminaries and small talk, when we were on our second drink, I asked him what his fantasies were.

His voice shook a little as he replied, which I loved – I love guys who are shy, I love guys who are nervous and shaky and unsure and even a little ashamed of what turns them on right down deep. 'I'd like to be tied up, and gagged. And I'd like to be beaten.' He looked down. I was intimidating him. I suppressed a delighted smile.

'It's all right,' I said, softly, 'that sounds just fine. I'm sure we can work something out. I have some specific plans, but I don't want to tell you too much about them.'

I saw him swallow but he didn't speak.

'I'm pretty sure, from what you've told me, that you'll like them,' I said, smiling the sweetest smile I could.

He exhaled, slightly aroused. 'I've never told anyone about this before.'

'Well,' I said, 'I'm glad you decided to start with me.'

We didn't hang around much longer. I had made my decision. I told him that if he wanted to continue what he'd started to turn up at seven on the following Saturday night, and expect to stay for twenty-four hours. He seemed both excited and terrified.

On Saturday, I spent a while preparing for his arrival. Softly lighting the bedroom. Positioning the cage so I could see it clearly from the bed and in the mirrors on my walls. No easy job as it was so incredibly heavy, but I managed to slide it along the carpet somehow. Then I put a plastic sheet on the floor beneath it and a soft fur rug inside.

I dressed in a close-fitting rubber T-shirt. It was comfortable and made me feel sexy. I teamed it with loose velvet trousers and flat black ankle boots. I was just finishing my make-up when the door bell rang.

Gem looked even more scared than he had in the pub, which I suppose wasn't surprising. He was wearing a black jacket over a black shirt and dark blue jeans, so tight I could see the bulge already stiffening in his trousers. I smiled, remembering again how perfect he was.

'You can leave your clothes in there,' I said curtly, pointing to a small wooden box which I kept just inside the front door, and left him to strip.

I was sitting on the sofa with a glass of wine when Gem came in, naked, his head bowed shyly. I nodded to the floor in front of me and he padded softly over to kneel there between my booted feet, resting his cheek sweetly against my velvet-covered thigh. Gem was naked and I was fully dressed – that made me feel so powerful and so turned on.

I took a collar from the coffee table and buckled it around Gem's throat while he rested, panting expectantly.

When the collar was in place I lifted his chin and kissed him softly on the lips then pulled away. 'Are you OK?' I asked, genuinely feeling the need to check in with him.

'I'm fine, a little scared.'

I smiled and squirmed around a little to feel how wet I already was. It had been a while. I had forgotten how much I loved this.

I waited a while then. Just staring into his eyes. I realised that I couldn't wait to see him locked in my cage, cramped and begging for release.

He gasped when I stood up quickly following my instincts. 'Follow me, crawl.' I led the way into the bedroom with Gem moving awkwardly behind me.

In the bedroom, I sat down on the bed. The clean smooth sheets felt cool through my trousers. Gem stopped at my feet, looking a little unsure what to do next. I glanced over to the cage and then back at him. I gave him a loaded look, my unspoken command clear. He swallowed, then crawled over to the cage and knelt expectantly outside the door. Standing up, I strode over and opened the door for him to crawl inside. I clanged it shut after him and snapped the lock shut. The noise of the padlock clicking home made me even wetter.

I sat back down on the bed then and spent a long time looking at him in the cage, his naked body lit by the soft candles in the room. He raised his head and as his eyes met mine I could see he was already begging inside for release from the tiny cramped space that kept him utterly exposed to my eyes. His cock was firm – hard against his belly.

A few moments later, and ignoring a pang of guilt, I stood up and walked from the room.

I left the bedroom door open so I could hear him if he cried out and sat down on the sofa to plan what I would do next. I had the boy in the cage just as I wanted. That alone was getting me so hot, but I knew there was so much more to go.

Images flooded my mind. I thought of straddling the cage and pissing on him while he was trapped beneath me. Or of watching him tease himself in the cramped little space. Or pleasuring myself instead, in front of him, enjoying the sight of his imprisonment and frustration.

A short while later, he flinched visibly as I walked back in. I ran my eyes quickly over him. His cramped body. His straining erection. I walked over and gave the cage a little kick. 'So do you like your new home, slave boy?'

'Yes, Mistress, if it pleases you.'

'That's good, but you know there's something missing.'

I crouched down in front of the cage and unlocked the small door in the front, which was level with his face. Opening it I took a ball gag and pushed it firmly into his mouth. It had a locking device that he wouldn't be able to remove.

And then I just looked at him again. I looked at him for a long, long time. Imprisoned. Silenced. And beautiful, so very beautiful.

I couldn't wait any longer. I slipped off my trousers and sat down on a chair next to the cage. I put my two booted feet up on the top of it, spreading them wide apart. My captive watched me with wide-stretched eyes. My naked cunt was only inches from him. He'd be able to smell it – see it glistening sticky. But it was completely unreachable. He couldn't even beg.

Reaching behind me, I grabbed my vibrator from by my bed. It was my favourite one, the kind that have an insertable piece and a clit stimulator. Twisting it to a low vibration setting I slid the larger section right into my wet cunt.

My prisoner moaned to see it.

'What?' I said softly, my voice catching a little as waves of arousal caught me. 'You wish this was your cock pushing into me?'

He nodded dumbly.

'Hmm, I guess you do. Shame you're locked in that cage, isn't it?' I moaned then, twisting the control on the vibrator to make it buzz faster inside me.

He made another frustrated noise, the gag preventing anything more intelligible. I bucked my hips so the clit stimulator slid snugly into place. Then I increased the vibration speed and sighed. I looked again at my

200

prisoner in the cage, trapped and helpless, staring at my cunt with his eyes wide above the gag. I thought about the fact I could keep him locked up for as long as I wanted. I thought about the fact his cock had been hard from back when I opened the front door.

I came then. Thinking about nothing more than his arrival. Scruffy and cute on the doorstep. And how little it had taken to reduce him to cowering, naked, prisoner.

It was much later that I let him out. It had been a long, long time and he was stiff and disorientated. I looked after him and thanked him and waited for him. I was a little nervous when I asked him for another date. But Gem smiled and nodded enthusiastically.

Perhaps next time I will pay some more attention to his adorable little arse.

– Cheryl, Leeds, UK

Valerie

If I say Miss Moneypenny what image comes to mind? An old bat wearing *pince-nez,* tapping a Remington in a dusty office with a hat stand in the corner? From the look of her pursed red lips you'd guess she has a fanny tighter than her hairdo. Or perhaps you can see under that ladylike exterior? Her – or *me* rather – wearing a tight blouse, buttoned demurely enough for sure, but with nipples wickedly visible, poking stiffly through the peach satin. You keep trying to avert your eyes, don't you? Don't want to seem impolite.

Am I taking a dictation in your fantasy? Because a fantasy is what you're having, isn't it? I can tell by the way you've shoved your hands into your pockets. Tell me again what you see. Am I crossing my legs very slowly so you can hear the swish of silk on silk, the squeak of upper thigh on walnut desk? Am I wearing knickers, do you suppose? Surprised I'm talking dirty like this? Well, you asked for a confession.

Now I'm perched on the desk, sucking the end of my pen. I raise my leg because you wanted to know if I was wearing knickers, didn't you? I'm always ready to help, that's why my bosses – Price junior and Price senior before him – treasure me. I'll happily offer a glimpse of the scented shadow beneath my skirt if asked nicely, show off the neat bush concealing my sex. I feel the lips parting now, like a little doorway, showing a shocking streak of pink, a little wet because you're looking and that arouses me. You're desperate to see this scented pink opening, aren't you? Desperate to feel it, poke it . . . *fuck* it. I just can't help using dirty words. So here we are in Price junior's office, discussing your difficult court case and all the while my cunt is resting on the blotter, maybe leaving a little smear as I shift and wriggle my bottom.

OK, enough teasing for now. Think this is all a cliché? The tight-arsed secretary, bringing biscuits, taking dictation, unpinning her hair, begging her boss to touch her? Well, let me press the buzzer and let you in so you can see for yourself how real it all is.

It's a haven in here, isn't it? That's my intention, to create a oasis for my bosses and their clients. I hated the place when we first moved here, hated everything – the view, the staff, the clients. I was on the brink of leaving the company, despite my perfect record of twenty years' devoted service. I was adamant. I couldn't stand all the glass. You can see everyone and everyone can see you. There's absolutely no privacy.

See the Gherkin over there? That forty-storey dildo rising into the London sky. I love it now, but there was a time I couldn't bear the sight of it. I preferred my old windowless oak-panelled room down in Mayfair, just me and my buzzer and yes, even a coat stand. But you can't beat this view. Every month or so the window cleaners spill out of the top of that gigantic multi-windowed phallus, attached to harnesses, and I lick my lips as I watch them. The sight reminds me of Junior's stiff cock erupting the time he caught me with Mr Franklin.

One day I'll tell him what I used to do for his father before he retired. I wonder if it will make him hard, hearing that story? How I dropped an earring at the end of the interview, had to scrabble on the floor to find it, found myself at his feet, saw the bulge in his immaculately cut trousers. How there was the smell of sweat and the hint of spunk in my nostrils and suddenly Senior was silently holding his penis and prodding its blunt end into my cheekbone. He tangled his fingers in my hair and pushed my face into his groin, tipping himself so that instinctively I opened my mouth and there was the sweet rounded end slipping stickily inside.

I was only twenty. I had never done anything like it before. But I didn't want him knowing that. He was already impressed with me and I didn't want to let him, or myself, down. I followed the slow movement of his body with my mouth so as to keep track of him, my lips clamped round the shaft. His hands closed over my ears so I could only hear the frantic rushing of my blood. I gripped the tops of his legs and kept the moist tip of his penis in my mouth. It jumped over my tongue, probing between my teeth. I opened my jaw wider. I had to please him. I had to have this job.

Senior's penis was engorged now and huge. I daresay the girls would say he was hung like a donkey. It was shoving and pushing down my throat, no attempt at control, going at me until I nearly gagged. I pushed the thick shaft back with my tongue, closing my lips around his length and sucking it back into the warm wetness of my mouth.

That's when I realised I was wet, too, between my legs. I didn't wear knickers, even then, so I just reached down and started fondling my own pussy while I sucked him. His penis stiffened and swelled even more inside my mouth and, as I sucked on it, I felt so proud. It was the first time I'd seen let alone touched or sucked a penis, and here was a stiff male organ nudging down my throat, and Senior's obvious, thrusting pleasure was turning me on, too. I could taste the salty droplets oozing through the slit as he thrust against the roof of my mouth. His hands dragged my head up and down the length of his shaft, more roughly now, yanking at my hair. I was his, his sex toy, and he'd never want to be without me. My mouth became loose, sliding up and down his penis, my slippery lips losing their grip. I was getting pins and needles in my legs. I started to bite instead, my jaw quivering with exhaustion as I nipped the taut surface, no idea if it would hurt him.

He moaned and groaned and shoved it in more roughly, spreading his thighs to get a better angle. My lipstick was smudged all over it, wet with saliva and his sticky juice. He had hold of my head and was thrusting harder, making me dizzy, using my face like, well, like a vagina, and he was my boss, my master. I sucked him, pleasured him while my own pleasure dribbled under my fingers, and then suddenly his cock stiffened, seemed to grow even bigger! I loosened my throat to let him in and he pumped once, twice, straining so hard down my throat that he knocked my head against the leg of the desk. I bit hard on him as hot spunk shot down my throat and he later told me that it was the way I bit him, more than anything, that clinched the job. It showed that deep down, I was the one in charge.

That's how I know Senior had a magnificent cock. Except I always called it his penis, not cock. Because he was older, you know. It was easier in the old office before open plan and brainstorming and networks and emails, where there were closed doors and blinds on the windows and IN CONFERENCE signs. But Senior brought his old mahogany desk here so I could hide under there and service him as required. Once I did it John

205

Prescott-style, got down on all fours, difficult in these tight skirts, and sucked his cock while he was talking to a QC. The QC couldn't see, but I imagined some guys over in the Gherkin could. I made a big show for their benefit. Flipped my tongue out so they could see how long and pointy it is, licked my lips, angled his penis into my open mouth and lapped it real slow. It gave me an orgasm to think of a couple of management consultants, or whatever, over in that big dildo of an office block watching me and rubbing their crotches while I sucked my boss's big fat penis.

Sorry, did you ask who Mr Franklin is? He was the client who changed my job description, if you like, from cocksucker, you might say, to . . . well, you decide. I've told you how with all these glass walls there's no privacy anywhere in this office? I'm lucky, actually, because being the big boss's PA I get my own little suite up here, including a bathroom. It's because I work such long hours, you see, and Junior never knows when he'll need me. Day or night.

So it wasn't long after we'd moved here and I was still sulking. Big time, as Junior says. I kept threatening to leave. I didn't like all this glass. I didn't like the noise. I didn't like the water coolers, or the fact that I had to walk past miles of cramped work stations like so many battery chicken cages just to boil the kettle.

Junior needed to butter me up, and he got his father in to help. He knew that would work. Senior could get an erection just from watching me walk across his Persian rug. He's the one who ordered me *never* to change my style, which is why I still wear these pencil skirts, high-heeled platforms and pussycat bow blouses. And guess what? I'm top fashion now! So Senior came in, crooked his finger, just like he used to, and I was down there, like a doggie, bottom in the air, nuzzling up between his legs, undoing his flies, licking his balls, taking out that incredible cock and sucking it, biting it and sucking it, having to feel between my own legs because it's so sexy when you're hidden, when it's forbidden. That's why, darling, I don't wear knickers. He was quick about it and I needed to touch myself while I sucked him, needed my own pleasure, my own relief, while he came, bursting and spurting into my mouth. He's sixty but he can knock his son into a cocked hat. It's rare he does it now. Maybe twice a year for old times' sake. It's only ever been oral, you understand. Except for the once. That way he's not strictly speaking unfaithful. Heavens, I'm his PA, not his mistress! Or I was.

Anyway, Junior didn't know how to deal with me. So father and son had a conflab, and they came up with the idea of the en-suite bathroom. And a little sitting area, too, with a sofa, where I can put my flowers and my scented candles for when I work late. I told you, I want my clients, his clients, their clients, whatever, to feel right at home whenever they come in here.

And so I was happy with my own little domain, and I agreed to stay. I could fret no more about my lack of privacy, because I wasn't having to reapply my lipstick and do my hair in the toilets six times a day (I wee a lot – it's all that coffee, and other things) with all those giggling secretaries and pretend to giggle at their antics or, horror, having to listen to them peeing on the other side of a flimsy cubicle wall.

No, I had my own bathroom, all very modern with glass bricks and ferns and spotlighting, but private. So private that I could come in here, still can obviously, walk across my office, past this glass brick wall here and into the loo without even shutting the door because those battery hens can't see me now!

Well, of course I thanked Senior *very* effusively for my special treat. When everyone had gone I shut the door, fairly useless gesture as anyone could have seen us through the glass wall, undid a couple of buttons as usual, so he could see the lace bra straining over my breasts, then I got down on my knees in front of him, saying thank you all the while, and started to push his thighs open. It had to be quick because I needed to pee. But he pushed me face down on my new little raspberry damask sofa, came up behind me, unzipping his flies, and without a word thrust his penis up my bottom. My *bottom*. I was shocked. How dirty! How base! Instinctively I tried to jerk away but he's so strong, and he was forcing his way up me, hard and fast. Apparently married men feel it's not strictly unfaithful if they fuck their PAs up the arse. Same as coming in their PAs' mouths. My bladder was swelling, the urge to pee was sudden and urgent, his penis was banging against it, and the urge to pee was enhancing all the other sensations. I mean, I was all closed against him at first, like a fist, it felt sore and yes, I was so ashamed at what was happening, especially as I thought I was going to wet myself, but this was Senior, he could do what he liked and I couldn't interrupt him. Anyway the surging burning sensation in my bladder was amazing, pushing, filling me with urgency. His penis was inside me, thrusting, thrusting, and then I was moving with him, his body hot through his suit, pressed hard behind me, and what was even more shocking was how good it felt. I was so tight – yes a tight-arse, just as everyone supposes – and he fitted in there, forcing me to open to him, feeling huge in there.

Then he came. And so did I, but as I did I felt the first hot drops of wee on my legs. I crawled away from him, red with shame, and as I dashed into my sparkling new bathroom I heard him say, 'That'll be all, Valerie.'

So you see, I may say I was happy with everything, but without my regular fellatio appointments with Senior I knew I'd become frustrated. There was no sex at home. I'm what they used to call a spinster. So I wondered, when I came into work the next morning and knew he had retired for good, whether a bloody bathroom to go with my office, however glitzy, was going to be enough. In fact I got a little angry, thinking about it. I paced about that morning, trembling as I thought about what had happened the night before, I couldn't believe he'd done that to me and left me, as always, wanting more. You see, the more I got the more I wanted. I'd been pleasuring him up to twice a day until then, but all it did was make me hungrier. I was a smouldering volcano. Don't smirk. You're having trouble believing this? You can't believe that a lady with perfect fingernails, a creaseless blouse and highly polished shoes takes it up the arse? That these Dior-painted lips, always the same classic red shade, used to wrap themselves around the veiny penis of one of the most powerful lawyers in town and suck it until he whimpered?

Well, haven't you heard it's always the quiet ones? I came in the next morning and found myself wondering how on earth I was going to continue working like the exemplary PA, with this gnawing longing driving me insane. I looked at the pile of phone messages on my desk, looked through my glass wall at the battery hens all chattering away out there, gossiping no doubt about their boyfriends, one even opening her blouse to show off her new bra – or was it her new boob job? They were all crowding round and staring at her breasts. God! I even caught myself asking, after all the fuss I'd made, what was so great about privacy anyway? Now my life was too damn *quiet*!

On the other side of my room Junior was behind *his* glass wall, dictating with the new digital software that goes straight into my computer. Bless him, he hadn't even noticed that his secretaries were all flashing their tits, as they would put it. He works so hard. I worry about him sometimes. He was swinging his chair about, his feet up on the desk. He's a good-looking boy. Exactly like his dad in fact. Except I hadn't at that point seen him undone. Touched him. Sucked him, you know. Given him the special Valerie service, as Senior used to call it.

Just thinking about his father made me wet all over again. Thinking about the night before, how he'd only managed to get my pencil skirt up so far because it was so tight, how anyone watching would think we were fully dressed, how I'd tried to stop him but he'd stuck his cock into me anyway, fondled my breasts through the satin of my blouse, pushed my nose into the sofa so I was light-headed, because I could hardly breathe as he humped me, roughly, almost violently, like the great dog he is. Fucked my arse until our knees were red raw on the carpet.

That'll be all, Valerie.

I bet you're wondering how low could I go after that? I'll tell you how dirty it gets. That next morning, when I was reminiscing about Senior . . . I think I was in love with him, you know? Yes, in love with him even after he took me like that, like a dog . . . *because* he took me like a dog. Anyway, I didn't know how I was going to go without. I paced about, making phone calls, unable to settle. I wondered what those secretaries were all bitching about. I went to my door but immediately wished I hadn't.

'Valerie the Virgin.' The girl who'd been showing them her bra said it. She swivelled in her chair. It was bubble-gum pink, her bra, cut low. She had no breasts. Pathetic. Something had changed in me. They could see it as I stood there.

'That's right, girls. *Intacta* and proud of it. At least I'm not a slut, like all of you.'

They just gaped, like so many goldfish. Are you shocked? That I lied? But yes, technically I am a virgin. In the mouth, up the bottom, they don't count, do they? So what you see is almost what you get. It's what makes me so attractive, *n'est-ce pas*? Everyone fantasises about a virgin.

I wanted to go on standing there but I needed to go to the loo. And I had to answer the phone. It might have been Senior. But it was just a client . . . and then another client. I couldn't help thinking about him, and the more I talked and cooed and soothed clients on the phone the more I thought about his hard penis thrusting hard up my bottom and the more turned on I got. I could feel my pussy squeezing ever more frantically the way it does when I'm pleasuring myself with my fingers, when I'm sucking Senior, or when I'm alone. The girls would call it 'creaming'.

At last I forgot about the girls and the clients and dashed into my bathroom. But by now I was so turned on that I couldn't go. Those girls would call it 'pissing'. I sat on the edge of the toilet and hitched my skirt up above my stockings. I tried to calm myself. But my pussy was pulsing with longing, kept opening and closing like a cross little mouth. I closed my eyes, tipped my head back and tried not to think of Senior. I spread my legs wider to straddle the bowl. It's so clean and white and lovely and new. I couldn't help myself. I had to shove my fingers inside me to bring me on, I was moaning now with desire for him, for myself.

There was that glorious pressing sensation again, the heat building in my bladder, then here it came, stinging, starting to rush and gush down me. As my fingers pinched and plucked at my sore clitoris and I moaned out loud, the drops of pee sprang out. I sighed as the drops turned to a hot thin trickle, dribbling over my fingers, along my pussy lips, into the crack, burning into all the open bits of me, running down my inner thighs.

'God, this is better than golden shower hour at uni!'

My eyes flickered open. Someone was standing in the doorway of my bathroom. My supposedly private bathroom. But now I was shaking as I tried to stop the piss coming. I could feel it, hot and strong, my whole body tense as I tried to stop it. The way I was sitting, my legs spread wide open, made everything more exquisite. And now someone was watching me.

'Go away,' I said weakly. It wasn't Senior or Junior.

'When the college girls came in from games – we called it golden shower hour! We thought we'd just watch them changing, but then they used to hitch up their little netball skirts and pull those big white panties down around their knees.'

'This is a private office,' I moaned as the trickle started up again.

'And I have an appointment. Oh, those girls. All smelling of unwashed teenage pussy and piss. It must have made them horny to know us grubby boys were spying on them, having an eyeful. I wonder if that lot out there are like that. What do you think? Doesn't the thought of it make you horny, Valerie?'

I tried to bring my legs together, hide myself, but it was too late. Instead I opened my eyes and stared at him. It was a client. Mr Franklin. Charming man, very ordinary, suit with tie askew. Fraud case. I said his name. He took it as an invitation and came closer.

'The door was open,' he said. 'But I could see you, straddling your toilet, all the way from the lifts. I'm sorry but I just had to come in and watch you.'

'I'll call security!' I looked past him. My door was open. My office was made of glass. The battery hens could see me. The whole world could see me. Or at least half the City of London.

'This casts you in a whole new light, Valerie. Not buttoned up Miss Moneypenny at all, now, are you? But still willing to please, I bet, because you're a dirty little tart. Look at you, wetting yourself. And right in front of me, too.'

He came closer and got down on his knees. He took hold of my thighs right at the sinewy top of my legs, dug his thumbs into the tender spaces just above my pussy where bone turned to aching flesh, pulled my legs open and pushed his face into me.

I gasped and yanked at his hair trying to pull him away, but he was already licking me, an easy thing to do the way I was spread open. The urine was gushing down me, the little valve open like a floodgate. Then the messy trickle started, spraying up and sideways before it focused into a neat yellow jet, a hot wet jet of piss arcing straight into Mr Franklin's face, into his hair, over his closed eyes. His mouth started opening. I couldn't believe it and my instincts were to stop the stream. But I had no control even if I'd wanted to – and besides it was too good, so dirty to be pissing into Mr Franklin's face, watching his mouth open up and my piss shooting in and dribbling down his chin. His lips were wet with my urine and he was actually swallowing it. I could see his Adam's apple jumping as he guzzled. I moaned again with the release as it went on and on splashing into his face. His thumbs dug harder and deeper into my flesh, milking every last drop. I wanted it to go on and so did he and I pushed my soaking crotch into his face as he drank my piss.

'Look what you've made me do.' My voice was shaking. 'You naughty, dirty boy. Puddles all over my nice new Roman tiles. What a mess, Mr Franklin. What would my boss say?'

'I want to lick you clean.'

Mr Franklin's face was wet with my piss. And so eager. I thought I was going mad. What indeed would my boss say if he could see me pissing all over one of our clients, who was enjoying it, asking for it?

'Always eager to please, Mr Franklin.' I started jerking my hips, and soon I couldn't stop rubbing frantically against Mr Franklin's face. He didn't have to do much. My pussy bumped his wet mouth and hard chin, spreading open on contact, making me moan again with pleasure. I pulled away.

'Let me lick you, Valerie,' he begged.

'Go on, then, Mr Franklin. Lick me clean.' I wriggled forwards on the lavatory seat and wrapped my legs round his head. He stuck out his tongue and started to lap at me. He slid it over all the exposed and stinging bits of me, adding his saliva to the other wetness. He made slurping noises as his tongue swiped over me. I spread my legs wider, wanted him right inside me, to get at the stinging, burning centre, and the only way in was with his tongue. I pushed harder against his mouth, letting his teeth bang and bite. His tongue ran up my red crack, the one I like to show my clients, teasing, peeling away the mystery little by little. The tip of his tongue flicked over my swollen clitoris and suddenly I felt like an animal, the soaring pleasure, the dirty guilty pleasure this was giving me. I rammed hard into his face, yanking his head up and down to make his nose and mouth rub harder, make him lap harder and faster, and I didn't know if I was clean or not but I came,

214

furiously, the pleasure jerking me about against his face like a rag doll.

He sat back on his haunches, watching me. I started to go very red. 'That was good, Valerie,' he said 'Now there's something else I want you to do.'

I closed my knees, tugged at my skirt. 'I really ought to get back to work. Mr Thompson will be here at ten.'

'Mr Thompson can wait. You want me to tell your boss that I just watched you pissing? He'd give you the sack, surely?'

I lifted my chin. 'Never.'

'Want to bet? The client's always right, isn't he?'

I started to stand up, but my tight skirt prevented me from straightening and I fell forwards onto my knees instead. 'They could never do without me.'

Mr Franklin laughed softly and tapped my bottom. 'That's how his father liked you, isn't it? His doggy. You think it was a secret? That QC told us all about it. All your clients have been longing to have a go since he retired.' He laughed, no longer begging me. 'Come on, Valerie. I thought you were trained to move heaven and earth to please your clients?'

'Didn't I please you just then?'

'Yes, but this firm's fees are extortionate. I need your service to get a whole lot more personal, Valerie.' He pulled a towel off the rail, flicked it. My bottom was in the air. He lifted my skirt up round my hips. I could hear the satin lining ripping with the force. Then he brought the towel down with a sharp smack on my bare buttocks. I gasped with the humiliation, the shame. And something else – the excitement! It was rising in me, so unexpected. Whoever heard of smacking being exciting? He smacked me again with the towel. I actually wiggled my bottom with pleasure. I started to crawl about in front of him, feebly pretending to avoid the slaps.

215

'How kinky is this!' He whistled softly, trailing the towel over my bottom, tickling between my cheeks with it. 'The ice maiden melts. Just wait till I tell Junior about this!'

'He won't believe you.' But I wanted him to smack me again.

'He can use his eyes. He's only over there, isn't he? Beavering away. Why don't we get him in here to see you waving your bottom in the air for me?' He raised his arm, and smacked me hard on the other buttock. It sang through me. My pussy clenched tight, making me gasp again. The hot glow spread through me, but the pain was turning quickly into pleasure. I even glanced over my shoulder to see, in the mirror tiles, my bottom with a red stripe across it. I wanted more.

'What can I do for you, Mr Franklin?' I asked, obediently, keeping my voice brisk and efficient even from my bitch position on the floor.

He dropped the towel and unzipped his trousers. His cock, I'll call it that, was already big and he was swinging it from side to side. There was a drop of liquid dangling off the end of it. He looked down at me. 'Your turn to taste my piss. Come over here.'

His cock jerked in his hand like some kind of creature moving of its own accord. I crawled across the floor towards him. He spread his legs, aimed his cock at me, and started. I remember thanking God my bathroom was tiled, not carpeted, as at first the piss sprayed in a hot jet onto my face, bouncing off my shoulders, soaking my shirt, but then I grabbed his hips, opened my mouth wide, and took it. I didn't taste it at first, just saw myself, the shame, the dirtiness, my client pissing into my mouth. How low could I go? As it shot down my throat and I gagged, forcing myself to swallow it, just as I used to swallow the creamy dollops of Senior's come, I started to thrill to it, the whole scenario, tasted it on my tongue, the salty acid taste, and something in me swelled with pride as well as this new, dirty excitement. As I gulped and moaned and swallowed the hot choking liquid, I even thought about how I might persuade Junior to add this service to Mr Franklin's bill.

At last the torrent slowed and he shuddered. 'God, you're hot, Valerie.'

I shuddered, too, breathless, my mouth opening and closing like the goldfish Senior used to have in his old office, Mr Franklin's urine dripping off my hair, soaking through my blouse so that my nipples stuck to the fabric and I sank down onto the floor feeling degraded yet oh, so liberated!

But then reality sank in again. The office. The glass walls. The time. The appointments. The fact that I was soaking wet, covered in Mr Franklin's piss. And as if to bring me further down to earth, the buzzer in my office went, and I could hear my assistant saying over the intercom 'You weren't answering, Valerie, so I've sent Mr Thompson right up.'

'Obviously business as usual, Valerie. I can see you're busy,' Mr Franklin said and laughed. He zipped up his trousers. 'I'll just show myself into the boss's office then, shall I? Oops, here you are, Mr Price!'

I looked up, my mouth still wet with piss. Yes, Junior was in the doorway, his cock in his hand. He was massaging it, his eyes staring at me. I could see the first spurt of come as he masturbated into his hand.

'God, don't waste it, man!' hissed Mr Franklin, pushing Junior towards me. 'She's like a bitch on heat! She's all yours!'

For the first time in my life I was unable to stand to attention. I was stiff, wet, smelling of piss, tasting of piss. I grabbed the towel and rubbed at my hair.

Suddenly I felt myself being shoved down onto my hands and knees again. Once more my buttocks were up in the air, cold and sore. The towel was still over my head. I felt hands on my bottom, and immediately pushed myself up higher. The hands spread my bottom cheeks wide open. I felt as if the skin might tear, could feel myself clench with resistance, but then the little hole started to soften, loosen, open, just as it did for his father, and then it came, Junior's cock, hot and hard, jerking uncontrollably as the warm jet started spurting into me.

I knew Mr Franklin was watching. I knew Mr Thompson was on his way. Maybe all the battery hens in their work stations could see. 'Go on, darling. Fuck me!' I whispered, reaching back to get at his cock, feeling it pushing up me. The excitement rising inside me again was electrifying. I'd never realised how my body could be used like this, every which way. How must I look, my skin red and sore from my own urine, my blouse soaked with Mr Franklin's piss, my bottom spread wide open as my boss screwed me, pushed and pushed and pumped. Young man that he is, he couldn't hold it very long and he groaned as he came, jerking me forwards, my face still hidden by the towel. Yes. While Mr Franklin watched, Junior oh so quietly – just like his father – fucked me up the arse and shot his load inside me.

I know you never tire of hearing my confession. So, Mr Franklin, how can I help you today?

– Valerie, Golden Mile, London

218

nexus

The leading publisher of fetish and adult fiction

TELL US WHAT YOU THINK!

Readers' ideas and opinions matter to us so please take a few minutes to fill in the questionnaire below.

1. Sex: Are you male ☐   female ☐   a couple ☐?

2. Age: Under 21 ☐   21–30 ☐   31–40 ☐   41–50 ☐   51–60 ☐   over 60 ☐

3. Where do you buy your Nexus books from?
☐ A chain book shop. If so, which one(s)?

_____

☐ An independent book shop. If so, which one(s)?

_____

☐ A used book shop/charity shop
☐ Online book store. If so, which one(s)?

_____

4. How did you find out about Nexus books?
☐ Browsing in a book shop
☐ A review in a magazine
☐ Online
☐ Recommendation
☐ Other _____

5. In terms of settings, which do you prefer? (Tick as many as you like.)
☐ Down to earth and as realistic as possible
☐ Historical settings. If so, which period do you prefer?

_____

☐ Fantasy settings – barbarian worlds
☐ Completely escapist/surreal fantasy

- ☐ Institutional or secret academy
- ☐ Futuristic/sci fi
- ☐ Escapist but still believable
- ☐ Any settings you dislike?

_____

- ☐ Where would you like to see an adult novel set?

_____

6. In terms of storylines, would you prefer:

- ☐ Simple stories that concentrate on adult interests?
- ☐ More plot and character-driven stories with less explicit adult activity?
- ☐ We value your ideas, so give us your opinion of this book:

_____

_____

_____

7. In terms of your adult interests, what do you like to read about? (Tick as many as you like.)

- ☐ Traditional corporal punishment (CP)
- ☐ Modern corporal punishment
- ☐ Spanking
- ☐ Restraint/bondage
- ☐ Rope bondage
- ☐ Latex/rubber
- ☐ Leather
- ☐ Female domination and male submission
- ☐ Female domination and female submission
- ☐ Male domination and female submission
- ☐ Willing captivity
- ☐ Uniforms
- ☐ Lingerie/underwear/hosiery/footwear (boots and high heels)
- ☐ Sex rituals
- ☐ Vanilla sex
- ☐ Swinging

☐ Cross-dressing/TV
☐ Enforced feminisation
☐ Others – tell us what you don't see enough of in adult fiction:

_____
_____
_____

8. Would you prefer books with a more specialised approach to your interests, i.e. a novel specifically about uniforms? If so, which subject(s) would you like to read a Nexus novel about?

_____
_____
_____

9. Would you like to read true stories in Nexus books? For instance, the true story of a submissive woman, or a male slave? Tell us which true revelations you would most like to read about:

_____
_____
_____

10. What do you like best about Nexus books?

_____
_____

11. What do you like least about Nexus books?

_____
_____

12. Which are your favourite titles?

_____
_____

13. Who are your favourite authors?

_____
_____

14. **Which covers do you prefer? Those featuring:**
    (Tick as many as you like.)

☐ Fetish outfits
☐ More nudity
☐ Two models
☐ Unusual models or settings
☐ Classic erotic photography
☐ More contemporary images and poses
☐ A blank/non-erotic cover
☐ What would your ideal cover look like?

_____

15. **Describe your ideal Nexus novel in the space provided:**

_____
_____
_____
_____

16. **Which celebrity would feature in one of your Nexus-style fantasies? We'll post the best suggestions on our website – anonymously!**

_____

THANKS FOR YOUR TIME

Now simply write the title of this book in the space below and cut out the questionnaire pages. Post to: Nexus, Marketing Dept., Thames Wharf Studios, Rainville Rd, London W6 9HA

Book title: _____

NEXUS NEW BOOKS

NEIGHBOURHOOD WATCH
Lisette Ashton

Cedar View looks like any other sleepy cul-de-sac in the heart of
suburbia. Trees line the sides of the road. The gardens are neat
and well maintained. But behind the tightly drawn curtains of
each house the neighbours indulge their lewdest and bawdiest
appetites. It's not just the dominatrix at number 5, the swingers
at number 6, or the sadistically sinister couple at number 4 who
have secrets. There's also the curious relationship between the
Smiths, the open marriage of the Graftons, not to mention the
strange goings-on at the home of Denise, a woman whose lust
seems never to be sated. Everyone on Cedar View has a secret –
and they're all about to be exposed.

£7.99   ISBN 978 0 352 34190 7

To be published in August 2008

INDECENT PURSUIT
Ray Gordon

When young and sexually vivacious Sheena is dumped by her
snobbish older boyfriend, she decides to get her revenge. So using
her sexual prowess she sets out to seduce his three brothers. Her
lewd language and loose behaviour prove irresistible to the men
and before long she has bedded them all. But her goal of
marrying into the wealthy family remains as distant as ever. In
desperation, Sheena sets her sights on the father; but 'the Boss',
as he is known by his sons, is determined to regain his family's
honour and at the same time teach the wanton young woman a
lesson in respect.

£7.99   ISBN 978 0 352 34196 9

To be published in September 2008

THE INDULGENCES OF ISABELLE
Penny Birch

In her third year at Oxford, Isabelle Colraine is still indulging her private obsession with dominating girls. Unfortunately for her, others are aware of her predilection and are determined to spoil her fun. There's Portia, an upper-class brat who refuses to accept Isabelle's dominance, and Sarah, a mature woman who believes the right to dominate has to be earned with age and experience. But worst of all is Stan Tierney, an older man who wants to take advantage of her and won't take no for an answer.

£7.99   ISBN 978 0 352 34198 3

If you would like more information about Nexus titles, please visit our website at www.nexus-books.co.uk, or send a large stamped addressed envelope to:
  Nexus, Thames Wharf Studios,
  Rainville Road, London W6 9HA

NEXUS BOOKLIST

Information is correct at time of printing. To avoid disappointment, check availability before ordering. Go to www.nexus-books.co.uk.

All books are priced at £6.99 unless another price is given.

NEXUS

☐ ABANDONED ALICE	Adriana Arden	ISBN 978 0 352 33969 0
☐ ALICE IN CHAINS	Adriana Arden	ISBN 978 0 352 33908 9
☐ AMERICAN BLUE	Penny Birch	ISBN 978 0 352 34169 3
☐ AQUA DOMINATION	William Doughty	ISBN 978 0 352 34020 7
☐ THE ART OF CORRECTION	Tara Black	ISBN 978 0 352 33895 2
☐ THE ART OF SURRENDER	Madeline Bastinado	ISBN 978 0 352 34013 9
☐ BEASTLY BEHAVIOUR	Aishling Morgan	ISBN 978 0 352 34095 5
☐ BEING A GIRL	Chloë Thurlow	ISBN 978 0 352 34139 6
☐ BELINDA BARES UP	Yolanda Celbridge	ISBN 978 0 352 33926 3
☐ BIDDING TO SIN	Rosita Varón	ISBN 978 0 352 34063 4
☐ BLUSHING AT BOTH ENDS	Philip Kemp	ISBN 978 0 352 34107 5
☐ THE BOOK OF PUNISHMENT	Cat Scarlett	ISBN 978 0 352 33975 1
☐ BRUSH STROKES	Penny Birch	ISBN 978 0 352 34072 6
☐ CALLED TO THE WILD	Angel Blake	ISBN 978 0 352 34067 2
☐ CAPTIVES OF CHEYNER CLOSE	Adriana Arden	ISBN 978 0 352 34028 3
☐ CARNAL POSSESSION	Yvonne Strickland	ISBN 978 0 352 34062 7
☐ CITY MAID	Amelia Evangeline	ISBN 978 0 352 34096 2
☐ COLLEGE GIRLS	Cat Scarlett	ISBN 978 0 352 33942 3
☐ COMPANY OF SLAVES	Christina Shelly	ISBN 978 0 352 33887 7
☐ CONCEIT AND CONSEQUENCE	Aishling Morgan	ISBN 978 0 352 33965 2
☐ CORRECTIVE THERAPY	Jacqueline Masterson	ISBN 978 0 352 33917 1

☐ WHAT HAPPENS TO BAD GIRLS	Penny Birch	ISBN 978 0 352 34031 3
☐ WHAT SUKI WANTS	Cat Scarlett	ISBN 978 0 352 34027 6
☐ WHEN SHE WAS BAD	Penny Birch	ISBN 978 0 352 33859 4
☐ WHIP HAND	G.C. Scott	ISBN 978 0 352 33694 1
☐ WHIPPING GIRL	Aishling Morgan	ISBN 978 0 352 33789 4
☐ WHIPPING TRIANGLE	G.C. Scott	ISBN 978 0 352 34086 3
☐ THE WICKED SEX	Lance Porter	ISBN 978 0 352 34161 7
☐ ZELLIE'S WEAKNESS	Jean Aveline	ISBN 978 0 352 34160 0

NEXUS CLASSIC

☐ AMAZON SLAVE	Lisette Ashton	ISBN 978 0 352 33916 4
☐ ANGEL	Lindsay Gordon	ISBN 978 0 352 34009 2
☐ THE BLACK GARTER	Lisette Ashton	ISBN 978 0 352 33919 5
☐ THE BLACK MASQUE	Lisette Ashton	ISBN 978 0 352 33977 5
☐ THE BLACK ROOM	Lisette Ashton	ISBN 978 0 352 33914 0
☐ THE BLACK WIDOW	Lisette Ashton	ISBN 978 0 352 33973 7
☐ THE BOND	Lindsay Gordon	ISBN 978 0 352 33996 6
☐ THE DOMINO ENIGMA	Cyrian Amberlake	ISBN 978 0 352 34064 1
☐ THE DOMINO QUEEN	Cyrian Amberlake	ISBN 978 0 352 34074 0
☐ THE DOMINO TATTOO	Cyrian Amberlake	ISBN 978 0 352 34037 5
☐ EMMA ENSLAVED	Hilary James	ISBN 978 0 352 33883 9
☐ EMMA'S HUMILIATION	Hilary James	ISBN 978 0 352 33910 2
☐ EMMA'S SUBMISSION	Hilary James	ISBN 978 0 352 33906 5
☐ FAIRGROUND ATTRACTION	Lisette Ashton	ISBN 978 0 352 33927 0
☐ THE INSTITUTE	Maria Del Rey	ISBN 978 0 352 33352 0
☐ PLAYTHING	Penny Birch	ISBN 978 0 352 33967 6
☐ PLEASING THEM	William Doughty	ISBN 978 0 352 34015 3
☐ RITES OF OBEDIENCE	Lindsay Gordon	ISBN 978 0 352 34005 4
☐ SERVING TIME	Sarah Veitch	ISBN 978 0 352 33509 8
☐ THE SUBMISSION GALLERY	Lindsay Gordon	ISBN 978 0 352 34026 9
☐ TIE AND TEASE	Penny Birch	ISBN 978 0 352 33987 4
☐ TIGHT WHITE COTTON	Penny Birch	ISBN 978 0 352 33970 6

NEXUS CONFESSIONS

NEXUS ENTHUSIAST

NEXUS NON FICTION

- - - - - - ✂ -

Please send me the books I have ticked above.

Name ....

Address ....

....

....

.... Post code ....

Send to: **Virgin Books Cash Sales, Thames Wharf Studios, Rainville Road, London W6 9HA**

US customers: for prices and details of how to order books for delivery by mail, call 888-330-8477.

Please enclose a cheque or postal order, made payable to **Nexus Books Ltd**, to the value of the books you have ordered plus postage and packing costs as follows:

UK and BFPO – £1.00 for the first book, 50p for each subsequent book.

Overseas (including Republic of Ireland) – £2.00 for the first book, £1.00 for each subsequent book.

If you would prefer to pay by VISA, ACCESS/MASTERCARD, AMEX, DINERS CLUB or SWITCH, please write your card number and expiry date here:

....

Please allow up to 28 days for delivery.

Signature ....

Our privacy policy

We will not disclose information you supply us to any other parties. We will not disclose any information which identifies you personally to any person without your express consent.

From time to time we may send out information about Nexus books and special offers. Please tick here if you do *not* wish to receive Nexus information. ☐

- - - - - - ✂ -